House of Ezyron

House of Ezyron

PRINCESS IZUAGBA

ỌMỌDE MẸ́TA

Parrésia Publishers Ltd.
82, Allen Avenue, Ikeja, Lagos, Nigeria.
+2348154582178, +2348062392145
theeditor@parresia.com.ng
www.parresia.com.ng

ISBN: 978-978-54860-7-0

Printed in Nigeria by **Parrésia Press**

To my family
Victor, Nuela, Summer, Sky and Prize Izuagba.
For being the strength, I need to move forward.

Acknowledgement

First of all, I want to give God all the glory for making this book possible for me.

I want to especially thank my family for the unmeasurable support they have given me, especially my parents Victor and Nuela Izuagba,who never gave up on me even when I was afraid to move forward myself. My siblings, Summer,Sky and Prize for being Interested and who are partly my inspiration for the book.

I am ineffably thankful to the staff of my primary school, Rola International School, MKO Abiola Gardens Ikeja Lagos, especially the Headteacher, Mr Tola Kareem, for giving me my basics.

To the entire Jesuit Memorial College,

Port Harcourt for building me up from my primary school basics.

I want to thank the class of 2019 JMC pioneers for being my Inspiration as well.

To my friends; Munachi, Chinenye, Oghale, Alma, Nikechukwu, Nkechi and Damola, thank you for reading and correcting my huge blunders and thank you for encouraging me all the way with this Book.

I want to thank especially my uncle Uchenna Onyemaobi, his wife and family in Port Harcourt who supported me in every way during my long journey in JMC.

To my maternal grandpa Ben Ntiwunka, grandma Ann, my aunty Chinna, my uncles Chimieze and Ugonna, aunty Onyii; I thank you for always encouraging me in everything I do.

I want to thank the ever-smiling Mrs Azafi Omoluabi-Ogosi of Parrésia Publishers Ltd for accepting my work and making the impossible possible especially my editor, Amarachi Chimeka for her conscientious guidance and support for the completion of this work.

Thank you all for having my back and pushing me forward, especially when I was too lazy to move.

Thanks for accepting my differences and making me feel special.

Chapter 1

I was snoring in my sleep while in the throes of yet another horrific nightmare, which abruptly ended as I woke up screaming at the top of my lungs. This has to be the first time I had slept this long while enduring a nightmare.

Every night for as long as I can remember, I have always dreamt about an army of demonic lions guarding a huge door, and every time right before I find out what was behind the mysterious door, I woke up shivering.

I really have to stop drinking chocolate tea at night, right before bedtime.

I like to believe I was a normal thirteen-year-old girl who went by the name Annabelle Nguma. A mixed African child, my mum was from Ethiopia and my dad Nigeria, with three elder brothers, though two of them happened to be my stepbrothers.

The woman most people believed to be my mum was actually my step mum, and I really didn't like her but not as much as I despised my stepbrothers.

My brother Andrew and stepbrother Matthew, who we called Matt, were both sixteen-years-old, followed by James, who is the most annoying fourteen-year-old I know. He never lets me forget he is just a year older than I am. Matt and James are both dark in complexion, sporting tall, thick bushy hair. Sometimes, I thought about how their hair seemed to always swallow combs. My brother and I, on the other hand, are of a creamy chocolate complexion with curly brown hair.

I rushed into my bathroom, praying evil things befall James. It was 8:40 a.m. I was going to be very late for school, thanks to the annoying brat messing with my alarm. I rushed through bathing and grooming myself. Luckily for me, I had set out my clothes the night before—my favourite blue skinny jeans, a purple checked shirt and purple sneakers.

I rushed down the stairs with my backpack over my shoulders. Today was my grade's, school excursion, so it meant I did not need to carry school books or submit my assignments, all I needed was my jotting pad and pens. I was speeding through the house heading for the back door in our kitchen when my step mum called my name, I had almost made it out of the house.

'I thought you were ill.' She said with crossed arms.

I wondered who would have told her such fake news.

'No, I wasn't. James sabotaged my clock, and I woke up late and—'

'Enough, young lady! When will you learn to own up to your tardiness rather than always blame my sons? Unlike you, they're serious and in school right now.' She said with annoyance.

This was why I couldn't stand any of them. It still baffled me what my dad ever saw in this woman. I did the one thing I was known for in this house. Ignored her and walked out of the house. I knew it was disrespectful but I saw no hope in trying to be nice to her for my dad's sake. It simply was pointless. I ran all the way to my school which was just two buildings away, with the shouts of outcry from my stepmum echoing in my head. Great! My conscience would not let me be. I made it to school just in time, everyone in ninth grade was standing in front of our block. The name of my school was Mayspring Academy, and our principal, Mrs Eke, had made it a rule to wear presentable home clothes when we were going on school trips.

At the school gate, were my two least favourite teachers, Mr Ajaku and Mrs Ohioma. Mr Ajaku, was my Math teacher, a dark and tall man with a permanent flaring nostril and baldhead. He always wore a suit to school matched with different patterns of ties that made him look ridiculous. He hated giving out A's or a 100%, to students, even if it was clearly deserved. I found this trait of his very unfair, but I did not have the guts to tell him so because I preferred lurking in the shadows and avoiding trouble. Because, believe me, I was already too much of a trouble magnet, even when I had done nothing wrong.

Mrs Ohioma, my French teacher was a terrible teacher. She rarely spoke English in her classes, which I thought undermined the learning process. I know I am not one of the brightest students and it doesn't help my ability to learn, when some teachers hated me for no good reason. Mrs Ohioma made it clear she hated me with all her heart. One day, she had given me an F and tore my test paper. Whereas I was sure I deserved a B or 80% because I knew in my heart I had done my very best and aced the test, but I guess there was no hope trying to win their messed up hearts.

As I get closer to where my class mates are hurdled up, I heard someone call my name and I looked around until I saw one of my best friends, Mara smiling and waving me over. I gave her a smile in return and uneasily hurried over, so no one would pay attention to me.

Mara, is Ghanaian and creamy chocolate in complexion like me, although she is shorter, average heighted. Her eyes are big and mouth small, which made her face look like that of a baby. Her shoulder-length black hair is pulled into a ponytail.

Mara was mildly mysophobic, her entire family was, they were all afraid of germs, and were all neat freaks. Everyone in her family wore glasses and her elder twin sisters, Maya and Mauna were very protective of her, because she could become very sensitive. Mara and I had instantly become friends in our first year at Mayspring and I knew without a doubt that we would become best friends.

'Hey Mara,' I said, once I got close enough.

'Annabelle, you won't believe what just happened today—' she said, jumping up and down but was interrupted when a familiar voice said from behind me 'Whoa, cool down, your undies aren't on fire, are they?' I turn around and saw one of my other best friends, Zoe.

I didn't always think of Zoe as one of my best friends, because most times than not she was a nuisance. Unlike Mara and I, she was light in complexion. Her dad was Egyptian while her mum was Indian. They used to live in the United States but they had to move because Zoe's father had gotten promoted and transferred to become the head of his company's Nigerian branch.

Zoe's short red hair was a bit messy. She was wearing black torn jeans with a black and red short-sleeved crop top, she had tied a denim jacket around her waist and was wearing a pair of black sneakers on her feet. She also was wearing her many weird bracelets with little bones on her wrists and the golden locket on her neck, which she never showed us what was inside.

Zoe was the only child in a family that was very rich. She had serious anger issues and was mostly passive aggressive. She was the bravest amongst us but also a serial troublemaker, she and Mara were the same height, which made me feel weird around them because I was gigantically tall, but I had no choice but to live with it.

'What are y'all talking about?' Zoe asked us, her American accent still very pronounced. Her accent stood out like a sore thumb, she had been born in and lived in the United States for ten years. We became somewhat friends during my first year when someone from the opponent team had slammed the ball into my face during volleyball practice in P.E. she had immediately come to help me out and that was that.

'Oh, I was telling Annabelle about something great that happened to me this morning,' Mara said with a squeak in her voice. 'Yet, she's still waiting.' I said reminding her.

Mara tended to forget things when she got too excited. 'Oh right, my dog, Lady, you know her. She's big with white soft fur and big eyes and…'

'Uh, just get on with it, you're making me sick,' Zoe interrupted.

'Right, well, she gave birth to three pups. Isn't that awesome?' Mara said, squealing. I am still surprised she took Zoe's comment in stride just like that. Maybe this was great news for her.

'That's so great. More dogs. Yay!' Zoe said but Mara did not catch the sarcasm. Mara had an obsession for dogs, her dad never told her no, so she already had eight dogs, but with these puppies that would make eleven.

'I know right. Group hug!' Mara happily shouted, pulling Zoe and I into a tight big hug.

We were able to free ourselves from her tight grip before she suffocated us. For such a germaphobe, her love for dogs baffled us and her lack of boundaries when it came to people she was close to.

The bus arrived as Zoe and I were recovering. Mara still excited started jumping 'Finally, the bus is here! Let's quickly get on so we can claim the back seats!' She loudly exclaimed as she rushes towards it.

'Let's hurry and catch up with her before she hurts herself,' I told Zoe and we laughed over it. We entered the bus Mara had gotten on, and I spotted her at the back waving at us to come and join her, she had saved us seats. There were two buses that would be taking us to the location and the teacher in charge of my bus was Mr Ajaku, between him and Mrs Ohioma, I would always select him, as he was the lesser of two evils.

The back row could seat five students and talking to each other in the remaining two seats were my other two best friends, Mike and Zina. Who were too engrossed in their conversation to notice us. My heartbeat had gone up and my excitement increased when I saw Zina. I had developed a crush on him, which now led to me acting weird anytime I was around him.

Zina was an albino. He was very cautious about the sun, yet he still had brown spots on his arms and legs, and a few on his face. His eyes were bigger than that of most albinos I had seen. He was wearing a black hat over his brown messy hair that usually covered one eye, a blue and white-striped t-shirt with a black leather jacket and blue jeans. I could not see what shoes he had on but that did not matter.

Zina was one of the very popular kids, and he also came from a rich home. His parents were Tanzanians and he had a little brother. He was very kind, generous, and he played basketball. Mike had always been his best friend ever since they were little. Mike was dark in complexion with shoulder-length black dreadlocks. He also was from a rich home and equally as popular as Zina. Despite the boys being tall, they still weren't as tall as I was.

Unlike Zina, Mike played both soccer and basketball. He was very charming so everyone couldn't help but like him, but I still found him irritating because he was very self-centred and could be extremely lazy at times. His mum was Nigerian while his dad was from Botswana. I first became friends with them when Mike and I became science partners, and Zina decided to help us a little whenever he was over at Mike's house and we were working on our project. It was fun.

I sat next to the window and Mara, because I hated sitting in the middle for it brought about too much attention. Zoe sat in the middle, between Mara and the ever-talking parrot, Mike.

'Hey guys, we're here.' Mara called out.

The boys stopped talking and turned to face us, I immediately made eye contact with Zina, who smiled; It didn't last long because I quickly looked out of the window. Why did Mara do that? I felt like a complete idiot right now.

'Hey Zoe, is it me or did a bird attack you this morning?' Mike asked referring to Zoe's messy hair. He began laughing at his stupid joke, and I looked back at them wanting to see how this one would end.

'Nah, I just had a bad hair day, but my pet vulture is looking for a new nest. Wanna volunteer? I assure you, she enjoys dreadlocks.' Zoe said smiling.

'Right.' Mike said with a new look in his face—disgust. Yet again, Zoe had won this round of their many verbal combats.

'Can you guys not even start? It's a bit too early, don't you think?' Zina said.

'He started it. Besides, he shouldn't have even tried it.' Zoe smirked.

Zoe found boys disgusting. Mike looked really angry and that was what Zoe loved, hurting guys with large egos. He was about to say something when Mr Ajaku cleared his throat to make an announcement. 'Alright students, during this trip, I would like if you all were calm and quiet. Any one of you that makes noise, shall have detention tomorrow.' He strictly said.

There's something special about today, Thursday, 16th of November. It just felt important and like a day I would never forget, but I think it's because it's a school trip and school trips were always fun.

'As you all know, we are visiting the National Museum today, in order to view the new exhibit for the deity named Ezyron, who was worshipped by a tribe that had been previously wiped off the map. But the discovery of new items have brought them to light and some of the items are now being displayed in the museum. After this excursion, the principal would like you to write a report on your experience and everything you will learn about this deity. Your report will be due on Monday.' Mr Ajaku finished speaking and sat down.

Immediately, everyone resumed talking. Teachers wasted their time when they bothered to silence students, it clearly was impossible.

'This is exciting. Do you know anything about the deity? I would like to know more. It all seems magical.' Mara said.

I felt the same way, but didn't say anything. The name, Ezyron, seemed familiar to me. My dad probably had told me stories about it. But I wasn't sure, only it seemed oddly familiar, but it couldn't be because prior to now, there had been no information about it. I rested my head on the window. I easily became emotional when I remembered things from when I was little, because my mum was still alive and my life was so much better and happier. The ride was going smoothly until I felt a hit from behind.

I let out a groan and searched for the culprit, when I didn't see anything, I was about to speak up, when Zoe let out a scream, she immediately cut off by covering her mouth as she didn't want to get detention, the others were still complaining when a hand popped out of the torn part of seat Zina was sitting on.

'Ah! It's a zombie!' Mara says loudly quite frightened

'Get real Mara, it's obviously a joke.' Mike said rolling his eyes. I found it funny how Mara's personality irritated him, like doesn't he look at himself in the mirror?

The tear on the chair started expanding and I knew our fear started to increase, when the top of a shaved head started to come through it, there was a bit of wiggling, but the head was stuck. To our surprise from under the chair came mischievous laughter, and the head disappeared from the tear in the chair and Nodebe, Zina's little brother, head came out from under the chair. I wondered how he had gotten there and unto the bus in the first place.

Nodebe had a small stature and was short, but his height was okay considering he was still growing and was the average height for most nine-year-olds. Like his older brother he also was an albino, with brown spots of various sizes on visible parts of his body, except his face. He was an intelligent yet troublesome child, who was always getting into trouble, where Zina had no choice but to come to his rescue.

'Nodebe, how did you get on the bus and what do you think you are doing here?' Zina asked his brother sounding extremely frustrated.

'Oh, no reason.' Nodebe said, his mischievous smirk in place.

'Why you little rat! No reason? Don't you have to be at school, instead of scaring the living daylights out of most of us?' Zoe coldly spoke.

'Most of us?' I asked with an arched eyebrow.

Zoe simply rolled her eyes. She believed she never got scared and was always trying to ensure people believe her.

'Well, I got bored. There was a fire alarm for about an hour, and Mr Mgba always gives a stupid long speech, so I snuck in and...' Nodebe abruptly stopped speaking.

'And?' Mara anxiously asked, wanting him to finish his statement. It was clear to all of us that she was still shaken from the scare.

'And that's all. You guys have no choice but to stick with me!' When Nodebe stopped speaking a full grin took over his face.

'Thankfully, we don't have to.' Zoe happily informed him, which immediately set him off because he angrily asked 'Why not?' and Mike rolled his eyes as he answered his question 'Because, we'll get into trouble.'

Mara being the goody two shoes amongst us, suggested informing Mr Ajaku, who unfortunately was on his way to the back of the bus and had heard the suggestion Mara had made.

'Tell me what?' Mr Ajaku loudly asked, scaring us. We all looked at him, and he had on a serious face, but for some odd reason his eyes were on me. I managed to sneak a peek at where Nodebe was talking from, but there was no sign of him.

He was such a clever kid.

'Um … ' Mara started and paused, because she was such a terrible liar, I prayed Zoe would jump in. She always came to Mara's rescue when it was important.

'Well Mara? I'm still waiting.' Mr Ajaku boomed, his eyes still watching me, like an eagle stalking his prey.

'She has a problem with her lunch, but she didn't want to disturb you.' Zoe finally spoke and I felt the tension in the air disappear. Mr Ajaku who was still looking at me started speaking. 'Well you shouldn't have bothered Mara. There's nothing I could do for you in this matter, as you were all informed to pack your food from home. If you all don't lower your voice next time, you shall all be getting detention without question. Especially you, Annabelle. I'm watching you.'

What had I said about being a trouble magnet, I hadn't done anything yet Mr Ajaku was targeting me out of all my friends, when I hadn't even uttered a word.

'Why did you help? I thought you wanted him gone?' Mike asks Zoe, who shrugs and said with a smirk 'He's just a little kid. As long as he stays hidden, we won't get into trouble.'

'Thanks Zoe.' Zina who had been quiet up until now, finally spoke. Mara came up with the idea of playing road games to pass time and not long into her first game, I start to nod off, her games are usually very boring. It felt like I had been sleeping for a while, when somebody shook me awake.

I instantly woke up, and the first thing I noticed was Mara's scared face. I wondered what was wrong.

'What's wrong?' I asked Mara, who shakily said 'The bus, it's empty. The others, Mr Ajaku and the driver are gone,' she was afraid, and it was clear in her voice. I had no need to stand up to verify what she had said. I saw the rest of our friends walking up and down the middle aisle of the bus talking to each other, they all looked the same frightened. Even Nodebe was no longer hiding. I finally noticed the environment outside, we were no longer on the main roads and It looked like we were in

a forest, because we were surrounded by trees and the ground was unpaved.

'Uhm, are we here?' I asked, even though I knew it was a dumb question, none of my friends bothered with responding. I looked back into the bus and every single person had also disappeared. My heart started beating fast and my panic was building I was trying to get a grip of myself, when something caught my attention. There was a shadow reflecting on my window, and what scared me the most was it had a weird shape that looked inhuman, but before I could really analyse it, it disappeared.

'You're just imagining things.' I muttered out loud to myself.

'You're all alone. There's no escape,' a creepy male voice that seemed to sound from within my head said, and tears started to fall from my eyes, as I held my head in fear, because I was already becoming crazy. I finally found the courage and released my head as I screamed the word 'No!' my courage left me as soon as it came when a huge hand slammed against the window beside me.

I slowly looked out of the window to see who the hand belonged to, hoping it was somebody that could help me. Looking at me was a light man with a bushy moustache and spiky short hair. I immediately started shouting for help, especially when I realized I was paralysed. But the man didn't move and he kept watching me, when I noticed under the bushy moustache lips were sewn together. I started sobbing, because this wasn't right or normal, I wanted to run away and find shelter, but I couldn't, everyone had disappeared and now this man! As he watched me crying helpless, he brought up his hand which I hadn't noticed before it had sharp long dark claws, where his nails should have been and started ripping the stitches sewn on his mouth. Once he was done, his lips had holes, where the threads had been. A creepy smile graced his lips as he sunk his claws into his head. I flinched, but he didn't seem bothered or in pain. I watched as he tried to pull his claws back out but ended up ripping half of his face off. The scream that erupts from my mouth is so loud, I didn't know for a second it was me that was screaming. I was going to die.

He pressed his injured lips on the window and I watched as a forked tongue slithered out of his mouth and licked the window. It was disgusting and I felt bile rise up from my stomach. He leaned back and his mouth started to move and the creepy male voice started speaking within me again. 'You can't escape!'

I watch him thrust his hand back, and bring it back with enough force, to shatter the window. I can't stop screaming, because I am scared and I won't be able to defend myself as I am still frozen. He grew in size and his hand stretched until he wrapped it around my neck, his claws skinning into my skin as he began to strangle me. My scream became wrangled and my eyes closed, I was screaming and also struggling to breathe. I opened my eyes one last time and instead of seeing the scary man, I saw Zoe's face.

'Is she awake?' I heard Mara anxiously ask.

'Yep, she's starting to wake up,' Zoe says, with relief in her voice.

Everyone on the bus had their eyes on me, they all had this astonished look, as if they were just seeing me for the first time. Even the driver, a dark man who was bald was looking at me from the corner of his eye. It didn't help that everyone could see my face, being as it were that I was the tallest person in my grade.

'Annabelle, detention tomorrow.' Mr Ajaku shouts from his seat in front. Gosh I hate him, why am I getting detention for having a nightmare? I didn't know I was screaming and disturbing everyone's peace. I couldn't do anything but slouch and hide my face with my backpack.

Soon, everyone is acting normal again, and my episode at the back of their minds. I watch as everyone got caught up in their various conversations and activities, even my friends are making a point of acting normal, but I know they feel sorry for me, and I hate it. Throughout the trip to the museum, I shield my face by staring out of the window, not bothering to interact with anyone and my friends got the message, I want to be left alone.

The bus stopped moving and I could see we were at the entrance of the National Museum, luckily for us, there hadn't been any traffic on our way to Onikan, Lagos Island. I felt a tap on my shoulder. I sighed and turned to look at who was bothering me, It was Zina.

'Uhm Annabelle, I know you still feel embarrassed about what happened, but you really don't need to feel that way…besides, we're here, let us all make the best of our trip.' he calmly said, trying to cheer me up, which I find sweet of him.

The Museum is huge. Its cream, painted buildings were rectangularly shaped. In front of the building, there's a roundabout and some walls which are made out of stones. The formation of the grass and flowers on the roundabout looks nice. Mr Ajaku announces for everyone to get off the bus, I grab my backpack and join the herd. Ours is the first bus to arrive. The other bus would probably join us soon.

Once I stepped down from the bus and joined my friends, we all looked at Mr Ajaku, who we knew was about to address us.

'Listen up. You all know, no form of indiscipline is allowed or tolerated under my watch. Today you're not only representing yourself but your school also. I expect you all to simply put on your best behaviours, be quiet and don't stray away from this group. If you are asked a question, do not hesitate to politely answer. Don't forget any form of misconduct is an automatic detention tomorrow.' Mr Ajaku kept quiet for a short while after he finished speaking, so his words could sink into us, before he continued to say. 'Now everyone, line up in twos.'

Everyone immediately started picking a partner that would stand beside them, Mara started waving and beckoning me over. When I reached her, she linked our arms and excitedly asked 'Partners?' she raised up a hand for a high five and I enthusiastically responded 'Partners!' also raising my hand to her's.

Mike paired up with Zina, and Zoe with Adonye, a dark girl with low cut hair wearing a purple and white polka dot short dress and a pair of black leather boots. Apart from us, her closest friends, she was the only one Zoe could tolerate. Zoe was usually picky when it came to socialising with people. Mara and I were behind Mike and Zina, while Zoe and Adonye were behind us.

'Alright, let's move in an orderly manner' Mr Ajaku announced one more time and the chain started moving towards the entrance of the building, were a light-skinned woman with too much makeup on her face, black and brown braided hair pulled back into a ponytail, in a brown skirt suit and black pumps, waited to welcome us.

'Good morning everyone, welcome to the National Museum. My name is Miss Uche Igbeya, and I'm your guide for today. Today, we'll be touring our latest exhibition, the deity Ezyron, where I'll happily share with you my knowledge of Ezyron and the tribe and their customs of the deity's worshippers. Also, please note that photographs are not allowed inside the museum. Thank you and please follow me.' she finished her speech with a practiced professional smile.

'This is going to be fun,' Mara squealed beside me.

'Shh!' I hushed her, the last thing I needed was another detention added to my record, because if that happened the school would invite my dad and my stepmom.

Mr Ajaku remained behind us in order to watch our every move. We passed some sculptures with pierced noses and came across a hall with pictures of the history of Nigeria like the first secondary school in Nigeria, CMS Grammar School; The first President of Nigeria, Dr Nnamdi Azikiwe etc. We entered another room with a signpost titled 'Exhibits and artefacts of Ezyron' the exhibit room looked better than the other rooms, maybe because it was new. The walls were painted in blood red, with most of the exhibits were protected behind glass. In one exhibit were statues of people dancing around a burning fire, the enclosing painted dark blue to signify night time. Their attire looked like sacks, the men wore it on their waists to cover up their genitals, leaving them bare-chested, while the women wore the sack like clothing on their chests and waists, they were also holding calabashes.

Miss Igbeya stopped in front of it and spoke 'These people are known as the Waziris. They are not familiar because they were wiped off the map before the British came. Many believe that it was a flood that wiped them out. As you can see, they are performing a traditional dance known as the Fire Dance which is said to invoke the spirit of Ezyron, the deity of good and evil to protect their men who were believed to be strong enough to go into the Evil Forest, which was the lair of the deity and return as changed men.'

Miss Igbeya paused to see that we were following her and what she saw pleased her because she smiled and continued.

'From research, it was discovered that the ritual occurred once a year, because the people believed they had to appease their god for their wrongdoings when they invoked his evil side; so every year, they celebrated a festival known as the Golden Tribute, where the entire village offered something made of gold to the deity to appease him.' Miss Igbeya moved to point at a picture of people offering gold to a strange-looking statue.

The statue had three eyes and a lion's mane with two sabre teeth. While staring at the statue, I remembered someone.

'Mara, where's Nodebe?' I whispered.

'In the bus, don't worry, they haven't caught him, hopefully.' Mara said the hopefully as an afterthought, a worried look took over her face but she shook it off and returned her attention to Miss Igbeya.

I wish I could have done the same, but all of a sudden, I no longer could hear Miss Igbeya. I had a strange sense of deja vu, like I had been here or should know about Ezyron, something mostly hadn't felt right, since I stepped into the room. I was looking around when I spotted a closed door at the other end of the room, which for some reason was odd to me. I was about to nudge Mara and point out the odd door, but decided against it, because Mara didn't like distractions while learning. I turned towards the boys and tapped Zina on the shoulder, both him and Mike put their attention on me and titled their heads up a bit to look at my face.

'Look at that door.' I pointed at the odd door at the other side of the room. 'It's probably another exhibit or a door to the next room.' Zina said, he clearly didn't find it as odd as I did.

'It's not right. I saw an archway at the other end of the room, that led to the next room.' I said, positive that the door was out of place here.

'Um…do you want me to ask?' Zina asked, and I simply nodded.

I never had the courage to speak up in front of people, especially adults. My friends knew this and always spoke or asked questions on my behalf. Zina rose his hand up, and immediately caught Miss Igbeya attention.

'Yes, you with his hand up. A question?' She said.

'Yes. Where does the door at the end of the room lead to? Does it have more to do with the Waziris?' Zina asked.

Miss Igbeya balked at his question, but immediately recovered and answered him 'Sorry young man, the room is out of bound.'

Why would they put a room that's out of bound in a very visible place?

Zoe was staring at me and I probably wasn't doing a good job at hiding my disbelief at the answer Miss Igbeya gave, and asked on my behalf again 'Why is it out of bound?' not bothering to raise her hand.

'No more questions about the door.' Miss Igbeya haughtily instructed us.

'That wasn't an answer, Miss.' Zoe argued riling up Miss Igbeya's nerves. Mr Ajaku wise to Zoe's antics decided to take over and put her back in line reproachingly said 'Zoe, enough. That isn't part of the lesson. Be quiet or get detention!'

Zoe wasn't a person that could be easily deterred and still persisted 'But we're supposed to learn about everything in this room, which includes what's behind door, right?'

It always amazed me how Zoe could talk back at teachers, even though I knew she was pushing her luck, it was a great feeling knowing she had silenced Mr Ajaku. Zoe started walking towards the door, which was very bold even for her.

'Young lady, stop right there!' Miss Igbeya shouted at Zoe who shouted back in response 'Make me!' We all watched in surprise as Zoe increased her pace and Miss Igbeya hurried after her, her displeasure written all over her face.

Miss Igbeya was angry and loudly said to Zoe 'Young lady return back to your class mates this instance!' but it didn't sound like her because her voice got distorted and became deeper. I felt like I was losing my mind because not only was it scary, no one else seemed to have heard the distortion, as they were all cheering on and laughing at Zoe's antics, while Mr Ajaku was trying his best to restore order.

Miss Igbeya caught up with Zoe before she could reach the door and dragged her back to where the rest of us were. Zoe forcefully removed her arm from Miss Igbeya grip and angrily walked back towards up, her face now a deep red colour.

'Why did you have to do that Zoe?' Mara asked, disapproval stamped all over her face, always the goody two shoes.

'To prove a point and I did it quite well. Didn't you hear her? There is something weird going on, with her and that room she's protecting.' Mara still annoyed responded to Zoe's answer with another question and sly comment. 'What do you mean? How would I have heard a thing through the talking that you caused.'

Wanting to diffuse the situation before both of them start bickering at each other, I spoke up 'I did. You're right, Zoe. There is something strange about her.'

'Really Annabelle, you are on her side?' Mara stated in shock. Of course, I was on Zoe's side, but I kept quiet, instead of giving her a response, everyone stopped talking to one another. It took a minute for the class settle down . Mr Ajaku apologized and calmed Miss Igbeya so she could continue the lecture and tour about the Waziris.

A while after the spectacle that had occurred, the remaining students who had been on the other bus came into the room, with Mrs Ohioma and their tour guide a dark man in a brown suit and black shoes. His hair was cut short and the beard on his face was bushy. It seemed they had been touring another part of the museum, because once they entered the exhibition room, Miss Igbeya asked us to head to the exit.

On our way back to the entrance I came close to the forbidden door and from where I was standing I could make out some symbols carved on it, although what the symbols were I wasn't too sure. We were led to another room filled with images and sculptures of the deity Ezyron itself and it felt more like a place of worship than an exhibition in a museum.

'Welcome to the shrine of Ezyron. Most of these sculptures were done by the Waziris, which was later on discovered by archaeologists. The Waziris also made a few of the paintings on display.' Miss Igbeya excitedly shared with us, it was odd how she had gotten more enthusiastic about the tour now.

Mr Ajaku instructed us to form groups of six and once that was done Miss Igbeya spoke up 'You're free to explore the room and note down as much information as you can possible hold about the Waziris, Ezyron, paintings and sculptures in this room. You can read about each of the artefact from the placards below them. Please do not touch any of the artefacts.'

I wanted to explore on my own, so I broke away from the group I was in with my friends. I wanted to understand why this deity felt so familiar and I knew checking the placards of the artefacts would help me out.

I walked around and jotted down some of the facts, to seem busy and like an interested student, but I really was not paying attention, until I came across an image that was so familiar, I immediately got goose bumps. The content of the izmage was something I saw every time I went to bed at night, in my nightmare.

It was an ancient door guarded by demonic looking lions.

My heart was beating fast and hard in my chest as I looked down at the placard in below the image with fear but curiosity pushing me along. The door led to a place which was known as the house of Ezyron, and was of the popular belief that the deity Ezyron true form was safely locked behind the door in the image and was guarded by the lions, it's minions. It was also a big fear that he would open the door one day and release all his evil rage on the world.

I got chilled to my bones, I felt uncomfortable and scared. If this was a myth, why had I dreamt about it every night? Was I becoming crazy? Out of nowhere the urge to touch the image became hard to ignore and I touched the frame of the picture, it was odd, it was very hot to the touch, which it shouldn't have been, the room was heavily air conditioned. I looked around, everyone was busy doing their own exploring while Miss Igbeya and Mr Ajaku were talking with one another. I turned back to the painting and quickly felt the glass on the frame and removed my hand, but that was all it took.

The moment I touched it, the glass started to crack and before I could blink it shattered and the glass went flying everywhere, I went down protecting myself from the shards with a scream. When I looked up everyone's attention was on me.

I looked up in time to see Mr Ajaku bring out a notepad and pen from his back pocket and began to scribble on it. He was probably writing down my name for detention, again. I wondered why detention would be more important than my welfare, a student under his watch? He angrily strode to where I was cowering before and asked.

'What happened here Annabelle?'

Wasn't it clear what had happened, I couldn't even speak if I wanted to, my body was still recovering from the shock of the glass shattering.

'Are you okay Annabelle?' Miss Igbeya gently asked, I didn't feel okay. While I was looking at her, her eyes started changing from brown to red, which further freaked me out 'Dear, I asked you a question. Are you okay?' she repeated herself forcefully this time around, wanting them to move away from me, I nodded my head in response.

'On behalf of the school, I apologize for our student's unruly behaviour and the damage that has occurred, the school will reimburse the museum of course.' Mr Ajaku started speaking once I confirmed I was okay.

'Annabelle isn't at fault here and the museum can replace the frame. Besides it was also believed that bad luck happened to people because of Ezyron and a broken glass was a sign from Ezyron that one hasn't paid a debt with him.' Miss Igbeya said addressing everyone who had gathered around us. A collective gasps went round the room which excluded Mr Ajaku and I.

She really had to be stupid if she believed that traditional nonsense.

Miss Igbeya started speaking again, but now her eyes had completely turned blood red 'Annabelle hasn't paid a debt she has owed for a long time.'

What could she mean? How could I owe a debt? Before I could ask her why she said such nonsense she grabbed me by the front of my shirt, pulled me up and slammed me against the nearest wall.

In her deep and distorted voice, which sounded like two people speaking, 'It's time for you to pay Nguma.' I was shocked to note the second voice sounded very familiar.

The voice belonged to the voice in my head and in my dreams. The grip she had on me tightened as Mr Ajaku came to my rescue trying to unhand me and move her away, but she turned her face at him and glared at him and let out a growl so low but extremely scary, Mr Ajaku had no choice but to move backward in fear.

I watched as my class mates and friends look on at me with fear in their eyes. Mr Ajaku turned to them and instructed them to move away and head for the entrance. Miss Igbeya watched as they headed for the entrance and didn't make a move to stop them instead she turned around to face me, but instead of a human face, she had the face of a feline.

I started screaming and tears fell down my face, when red hair in copious amount started to grow and cover her exposed body. Her clothes were ripped and red hair could be seen sticking out from where it was torn, her skin had turned to red fur and we were now looking at a red lioness.

She dropped down on all fours, there was no way I could escape, I had to pass her to get to the entrance and exit the room. To my horror she began to multiply in size to the point where she was taller than me and bigger than the average lion.

She watched me like a lion watched its prey and when she was about pounce on me, something red hit her on the head with a lot of force that had her releasing a deadly snarl and snapping her head in the direction before she passed out. It was Mr Ajaku, and in his hands was a fire extinguisher.

He grabbed me and started running, while shouting 'Run! Stick together!' We had to run to the first exhibition to alert the other students and Mrs Ohioma, who were surprised that everyone including Mr Ajaku was causing chaos.

'What's going on? What has happened?' Mrs Ohioma apprehensively asked Mr Ajaku, who was trying hard to catch his breath.

'I'll explain, but let's leave now.' Mr Ajaku said hurriedly trying to urge Mrs Ohioma towards the exit.

The male tour guide with Mrs Ohioma's group interrupted their discussion and said 'I'm afraid all is not well.' The exhibition room turned into chaos as different students started screaming in fear as the tour guide also turned into a red lion and immediately headed for me.

I guessed all the staff in the museum had to be possessed. The lion leaped when it was near enough to pounce on me, and I was frozen to spot in fear, I heard everyone screaming around me, but before he could land on me Mr Ajaku was in front of me and swung the fire extinguisher with all his might at the lion's head, which sent it crashing into one of the exhibits. I never would have thought, there would come a day I would be thankful and grateful for Mr Ajaku, who had now turned out to be my hero.

'Run! Get out of here!' Mr Ajaku was shouting, but everyone else was ahead of him as they had already started running towards the exit and out of the building.

I was behind everyone, but my friends managed to fall back and surround me, checking up with me to ensure I was okay.

'Why is this happening Annabelle?' Mara asked breathlessly 'I don't know!' I hastily replied, when we reached the door, we watched it slam shut and no matter how much we pushed and tried to open it, it wouldn't budge.

Mara screamed and started crying, which had Zoe hissing and narrowing her eyes in annoyance at her 'Shut up! you are going to wake them.'

'Mr Ajaku, can you hear me?' Zina asked loudly.

Mr Ajaku muffled response came through to us 'Yes. Hold on a bit longer and stay away from those creatures as I find a way to open the door, the police are on their way.'

While we were trying our best not to be scared and hold on to our waning hope we heard growling behind us.

'Are we going to die?' Mara sobbed out as we all turned away from the door to see the two large demonic lions growling at us. 'There has to be another way out.' Mike anxiously said. We all started looking around searching for a way out when my eyes landed on the out of bound door.

'That door. Let's go!' I said as I sprinted off, not waiting to check if they were behind me. The lions took off after me and attacked me from both sides, I don't know where the strength came from or I successfully did it but I leapt over them at the very last second and they crashed into each other. The crash was powerful it knocked them out once again and I was able to reach the door without looking over my shoulder, but my friends weren't with me, I turned around saw them running towards me, seeing as the coast was somewhat clear for now.

'That was awesome Annabelle!' Mike ecstatically announced when they were close enough

'Really, making bold moves Giant!' Zoe agreed with him and playfully punched my arm. I usually got offended whenever I was called a giant, because of how insecure of my height I was but this time, I knew she was complimenting me. I smiled at them in response not wanting to waste any more time being trapped in the room with the lions, I grabbed the doorknob, but when I pushed it down, it didn't budge.

'It's locked.' I dejectedly informed them.

'Great! We're still stuck!' Mike screamed in frustration. Zoe got a thoughtful look on her face before she spoke 'Or maybe we're not.' she knelt down by the door and dug her hand into her messy red hair and released a hairpin. She was going to pick the lock with it we watched as she inserted it in the keyhole and started to jiggle it around.

The lion started moaning, as it began to wake up once again, the tension in the air around us grew thick with fear and Mara stupidly said to Zoe 'Can you go any faster?' Zoe who was trying her best responded with annoyance 'That's if you stop disturbing and let me concentrate.'

'Does anyone have anything we can use for protection?' I fanatically asked them, taking off my backpack to search it, hoping I would by some miracle come across something in it, the rest also started doing the same thing.

My backpack was empty, I had nothing hard that could harm even a fly 'I've got nothing,' I said to them and Mike and Mara chorused my answer back at me, but Zina had something different to say 'How about this?' he asked as he tossed something up and down.

He stopped and presented it to us, it was a green apple. I smiled at him, because an apple really? But we really didn't have options to choose from 'It's worth a try.' I said and retrieved it from him.

I stood straighter and aimed the apple at the lion, who was watching us. I used all of my strength to lob the apple at the lion's head and it collided with its nose, with so much force the apple splattered everywhere and the lion let out a series of shrill whining.

'Nice throw,' Zina commented.

'You have a good arm.' Zina commented, which made me blush, I hid my face and avoided eye contact with him as I thanked him and turned to Zoe. 'Are you near done yet?'

'Still need a little more time,' was her reply, not breaking her concentration. I looked back at the lions, they were both awake, and they were slowly prowling their way forward. Mike noticing them also said to everyone 'We don't have much time.' He sounded on the brink of tears, there was nothing we could use to protect ourselves, until I spied something red, the abandoned fire extinguisher lying further away from us on the floor.

'I'll be right back.' I announce before sprinting off for the fire extinguisher. Ignoring my friends worried outcries. The lions seeing me heading in another direction changed their path and headed for me, after all I was the one who apparently owed them a debt.

The lions were quickly gaining on me, so I leaped when I was close enough to the fire extinguisher and grabbed it. Immediately the lioness leaped for me as she was faster and I didn't hesitate as I swung the extinguisher at it, back and forth, I didn't know how to stop swinging, I just wished she would stay down and not come and attack me or my friends.

I was caught up in ensuring the lioness stayed down, I forgot about the other lion, which was now growling behind me, I swung around to face it, I dropped the fire extinguisher in the process, I couldn't protect myself, whether I bent to retrieve it or not it would kill me. I closed my eyes and curled into a fetal position trying to protect my head, but instead I heard a repeated thud, I chanced a look and saw Zina heavily panting, he was holding another fire extinguisher and the lion laid unconscious at his feet.

Zina came to me and pulled me to my feet and hugged me, his heart was pounding as hard as mine was. 'We're okay.' Was all he said before he released me. I nodded my head, to shaken to speak just yet. 'C'mon let's go before they wake up.' He took my arm and we hurried over to where the others were watching us with ashen faces.

'I've successfully jimmied the door.' Zoe called out to our approaching forms with glee. Zoe gestured to the door and curtsied for us before formally saying 'Ladies and gentlemen behold,' and opened the door.

We all walked through the door to be met by surprise, because it was an empty room.

'What the—?' Zoe had started to say, when she was interrupted 'This is the Nigerian Police speaking, children hold on a little longer we're coming to get you.' A deep voice that could only belong to a man loudly announced.

We rushed out of the room, happy that our captivity was nearing an end, but we weren't expecting the horror that stood before our eyes. The two lions had fused together to become one giant monstrosity. It was extremely horrendous to behold, it had four large eyes, four fore legs and two hind legs, and a massive tail that look like it could break anything it touched. The lion faced us and let out a terrifying roar, I wet myself a little. In the chaos, the police bust into the room and immediately started shooting at the lion.

I urged my friends to drop to the floor, so stray bullets won't hit us and to start crawling towards the exist where a fair police woman was beckoning us over. I was at the back of the line, when I felt something hot and heavy clamp down on the back of my leg stopping me from moving. I turned around to see the lion looking down at me. It roared at me, the bullets from the policemen guns not having any sort of effect on it, it used his jaw to lift me with my top and threw me into the Waziris exhibit.

With a roar and swing of its tail it wiped out many of the police officers shooting at it before it started prowling towards me. It was bad, but I managed to pick up a discarded spear from one of the ruined Waziri sculptor, and once the lion was close enough, I pulled myself together and aimed the spear at it with all my might.

I watched it pierce through the skin of the lion and embed itself deep into its chest. The lion started whining, growling softly until it crashed to the floor and stopped moving.

I picked myself up, and limped my way out of the room and out of the museum.

I fell into the arms of Mrs Ohioma, who hugged and was smiling at me, which was very odd because she had never been nice to me, not to talk about smiling at me with relief. 'Thank goodness. You're alright!' she said in joy, her hold on me tightening.

Everyone was already on their various buses, which were on standby and ready to boot it out of the danger zone. Mrs Ohioma released me and urged me into my bus, where Mr. Ajaku was motioning for me to enter and join my friends who were also standing behind him on the bus.

The moment I stepped onto the bus Mara hugged me and my friends followed, engulfing me in a group hug, which had everyone else staring at us, we broke up and moved to the back of the bus to take our seats.

We sat quietly, engrossed in our various thoughts, replaying what had gone down, when the silence was broken by a little voice sleepily asking us 'How did the excursion go?' It was such a loaded question, we all turned to look at Nodebe, who was rubbing sleep from his eyes, he took us in and asked 'Why do you guys look like you were playing roughly?' I had forgotten about him, we didn't have the energy to answer him, and when no one responded to his questions, he went back to hiding, annoyed.

Once we got to school, the teachers reported what had happened to the school's administrative team, and an impromptu meeting was held, where they addressed my whole class about what had happened and handed us letters to give to our parents.

'Good evening Dad, I'm home.' I shouted once I got in. My dad was a chocolate coloured man with a full beard and a bald scalp. He worked overtime in order to provide for his family, who he did just about anything for. 'Hey Cupcake, how was the excursion?' he asked me as soon as he spotted me.

'Ugh…it was so horrible and scary!' I said as I took a seat at the dining. My father was surprised at my reaction and fully looked at me. 'Hmm, why are you being a grouch and why would a museum trip be scary?' he asked.

'The school trip was a disaster, because Ezyron exhibition,' I said.

Once I said Ezyron, my father froze and his eyes turned to me, a brooding look taking over his face

'Ezyron?' He verified.

'Yes, I thought I was going to die, there were demonic lions. The one who spoke to me said I owed a debt. They were after me, dad.'

My dad sat lost in his thoughts for a while, I thought he had forgotten about me when he spoke 'Annabelle, eat your food and go to sleep. Tomorrow, I'm taking you and your brother to visit someone.'

'Why are we going out tomorrow? I have school tomorrow.' I reminded him, but he shook his head 'No school tomorrow. Tell Andrew about the change of plans.'

It had been a while since only my brother, dad and I, went out together without the rest of his family. 'I love you, dad.' I said and went to my room and dropped my backpack, before I headed to Andrew's room. Just like every other older teenager, Andrew hated it when anyone invaded his privacy, so I always knocked before I entered his room. I didn't wait long because the door opened and his head popped out.

'Hey Annie, what's up?'

'We're going on a trip tomorrow with dad, we aren't going to school.' I said the last bit excitedly. The only person taller than me was my brother, and he had the body mass to make him seem like a giant.

'Alright, thanks for the heads up.' he said, holding his hand out to me for a high five. 'How was your day…the excursion?' I let out an insufferable groan, which had him arching his brows not expecting such a negative response 'Horrible. I'll tell you about it later, I'm tired.'

'All right, I'll wake you up for dinner.' Andrew said, I nodded my head in response and went back to my room. Despite him being older, we got along just fine. After double checking I had locked my door, I removed my shoes and changed into something more comfortable before I laid down on my bed.

You were just lucky, the voice said in my head. Why had dad not been really surprised and why did he suddenly want to go on a trip. I was starting to believe he knew more than he was letting on.

Chapter 2

I didn't want to eat whatever was made for dinner, because it was food made by my stepmum. Andrew and I usually ate out or ordered in, our step mum's cooking was terrible. Although, she had taken a cooking class less than a month ago, to improve because our dad insisted we give her another try, but for me her food was still horrible to the point I was sure I could cook better. Not only was she a bad cook, she was also lazy. Whenever our dad was away, Andrew and I did all the work in the house, while her sons did nothing but goof around, ruin what we had done or were off playing with their friends. We were maltreated, Andrew tried to take the brunt of it but, I was always her main target.

Dad was completely blinded by her fake charm and didn't listen to Andrew and I when we complained. Instead he kept telling us to be nicer to her. I calmly told them I wouldn't be eating dinner and would just love to sleep, my dad understandingly let me off easily to my step mum's displeasure. I didn't understand her, shouldn't she be happy I was starving and not eating her food? I took a pack of biscuit out of a cupboard and bided everyone goodnight.

I woke up with a scream as usual, my alarm hadn't even gone off yet. It was still very early, so I took my time bathing, brushing and getting dressed. I wasn't as early as I had thought because when I got downstairs my brother and dad were in the living room watching TV.

'Good morning!' I brightly said to both of them. 'Good morning, Cupcake, how was your night?' My dad immediately asked me, welcoming me with a smile 'Fine,' I always lied whenever I was asked that question because I never wanted my dad worrying about me. 'Are you both ready?' our dad asked us.

'Yes dad.' Andrew and I answered together.

'Alright, let's go to the car so we can be on our way.' As soon as dad finished speaking our stepmom came out from wherever she was hiding and started questioning him. 'Where are you going to? Why is it only two of them you're taking? They should be taking a day off from school?'

Dad smiled at her calmly as he responded 'Onye, it's a family matter, biko.' my stepmother face turned into a scary mask as she frowned bitterly 'Aha, so we're not family again, abi?' she asked, her hands on her hips. I felt like screaming 'NO!' and I could see Andrew was barely holding himself back from doing the same. Dad didn't say anything, instead he shook his head and instructed us to head to the car.

I was surprised he had ignored her, wherever he was taking us to had to be very important, because he never fought with his wife and always wanted her to be content. We left the house without any more drama. I wish I could have informed my friends that I wouldn't be coming in to school, but I was also relieved I didn't have to go because I would have been subjected to stares and people gossiping about me.

Our dad refused to tell us where we were going, so Andrew and I kept busy, Andrew sat in front in the passenger seat, so I had the back seat all to myself, which I took advantage of by lying down, I plugged in my earphones and listened to music as well as play games on my phone. Andrew had brought along his PS4, so he was playing a game. We were all silent focusing on our own thing, when I noticed what was written on a sign as we drew closer to it.

GOOD BYE LAGOS

I stopped playing my music and using my phone to ask 'Um, Daddy…why are we leaving Lagos?' Andrew looked up just in time as we passed the sign board.

'You don't have to worry about that, you'll know once we get there.' he dismissed my question, still being secretive. Andrew and I exchanged looks. Reaching a silent agreement to let it go.

The car came to a stop at a fast food joint and dad said to get anything we wanted, because we still had a long journey ahead of us. We ate in the car, I had gotten jollof rice and chicken, as well as a chicken burger, fries, a bottle of water and a bottle of Coca-Cola now that was what I called a feast.

The journey grew so long and tiring, Andrew and I eventually slept off, I woke up when the car came to a screeching halt. I hadn't slept so peacefully in forever and I was surprised, I hadn't had a single dream or nightmare, I was sad that I woke up. I groggily sat up and looked out of the window, we were in a rural environment, which resembled our village. Why would my dad take us to the village and not take the others along? 'Oh good you're awake Annie, we're here.

Andrew wake up.' My dad said once he noticed me sitting upright, he got out of the car, leaving me to fully wake Andrew.

I shook Andrew's shoulder, which startled him and made him proclaim 'I'm awake o!...Where are we?' He also asked taking in the environment 'The village,' I answered. 'What? Why?' he asked.

I shrugged because I was also clueless.

'Kids come out.'

Our dad called out to us, and we both got out from the car. The ground were an unpaved mess, and for buildings a few huts were strategically placed around. In the distance I spotted some young boys who had on dirty clothes playing soccer.

I turned back to my father and asked 'Daddy, so why are we here?'

'Stop with the questions Cupcake, you both should just follow me and don't talk to anyone. Understand?' I felt reprimanded but both Andrew and I replied 'Understood.'

We walked a short distance before our father stopped in front of a small hut, which was made of clay and had a roof made from thick woven thatched grass. The hut had two windows and a door, which had wooden doors attached in order to close them, but both the windows and door were wide open.

Dad did not knock and just beckoned for us to follow him as he stepped into the hut, removing his shoes. 'Kids remove your shoes and give them to me.' We did as we were told, and he dropped them at a corner along with his own. The room was small. There was a mat on the floor and the walls were decorated with what looked like idols and beads.

'Is this a shrine?' Andrew asked his puzzlement was very clear in his voice, beating me to asking the question. 'Oh yes, my child.' A dry, raspy but still audible voice responded. The voice belonged to an old woman with grey hair, who had a *wrappa* tied around her chest with different beads on her body, she left the entrance where she had been watching us and walked into the hut.

'Take a seat, my children.' She said as she pointed to a mat in front of us. Dad sat down first, so I sat on one side of him and Andrew on the other. I was a bit scared so I looped my arm with my dad's own. Once we were seated the old woman sat down on the mat that was opposite ours.

'Why are you here, my son?'

'It's about Ezyron.' My dad replied heavily. At the sound of the deity's name I froze and looked from my dad to the woman, while Andrew remained quiet and indifferent.

The woman looked at me with an equally serious face and asked in a solemn tone 'Did you pay it?' I watched our dad age before my eyes as he looked down ashamed and replied 'I couldn't.'

What didn't he pay and how did it have to be with me? Because the demons at the museum had said I was owing a debt and I needed to pay, if my father wasn't going to give me answers I would ask the old woman.

'Sorry ma, I went somewhere yesterday and I was attacked by demons in the form of lions, they said I had a debt I hadn't paid. Is this what you're talking about?'

To Andrew and I's surprise our father started to sob and we watched tears stream down his face before he hid behind his palms. 'It has to give me more time, it can't start now.' He sobbed out to us.

'Daddy what is wrong? Please what is going on? What did you do? None of this is making sense.'

Andrew spoke alarmed at how our father had lost himself. The old woman looked at our father disrupt form and spoke up 'I will tell you. It's time you both knew about Ezyron, and what it has been doing to your family.' She paused to check we were paying attention before she continued speaking.

'Children, I'm Madam Sarki. What I am about to tell you is very unusual, and your feelings towards your father, may never be same. Your father and mother were in love and got married in secret because your mother's parents didn't approve, but why they disapproved they didn't say. When your mother's parents found out about the union it was too late and they finally confessed. Ezyron had gifted them a child and in return that child had to be betrothed to him and to remain pure, untouched and never to be wedded to any mortal. Ezyron was furious and as punishment for the betrayal he made your mother barren.' She paused for a few seconds to catch her breath and continued speaking.

'Ten years went by and your mother could not bear a child and after consulting with your mother's parents, they knew the best decision was to plead with Ezyron. Ezyron was still furious but he agreed to give her a child at the cost of your mother's life. Your father did not accept and pleaded with your mother, to reconsider because her life was more precious and they could always adopt, but she refused. She wanted a child made from the love they had for each other, your mother ignored your father and agreed. Not a year had gone by, when a baby boy was born. Your mother was really happy, when she gave birth to you, son, but she wasn't satisfied as she also wanted a baby girl to call her own, so she went behind your father's back and begged Ezyron to spare her more time, so she could spend a little time with her son and the baby girl she wanted before he took her to the spirit world. Ezyron was no longer simmering with anger, so he accepted her request once again, after all she had been born to be his wife first.'

Andrew and I were in shock, I didn't know how he was taking the story, but I believed every single word Madam Sarki said, because of what I had experienced the day before, nothing was unimaginable anymore.

'This second request he granted also had a deadly price, in exchange for new life, he had to take one in return and so your father's life was bought. He said she would die when the girl, you, my daughter turned six. Once the girl was born, your mother began to fall ill, and soon after six years, she died, paying the debts of the first one. For the second debt to be paid, your father has to kill himself or you my daughter has to die. If not Ezyron would rise and not only destroy your family, but also cause havoc and destruction upon the rest of the world.'

I couldn't believe what the debt I owed was, a debt I had nothing to do with making, it was not making any sense how my mum would have thought she made a wise decision and also be the reason behind bad luck following me around like a plague.

'Don't fear my children, there's still a way out of this. To save your life and defeat Ezyron, the door of Ezyron, deep inside the evil forest, of this village has to be permanently sealed. Your father is an old mortal man, who can easily be killed by Ezyron and his minions at any time and place but you, the young children, especially the girl might have a chance of living—'

'No, the children shouldn't be involved in this. I'll figure out a way,' I hadn't notice my dad had pulled himself together and was silently listening to the woman as well, when he had interrupted and spoken.

'Please do you want harm to befall her once again? You know as well as I do that she is your last hope, in fact I thought you brought her here so I could properly instruct her on the quest she will no doubt go on.'

'Quest? I wanted you to be here while I finally told them about their history. I do not want to send her on a dangerous mission.' He shook his head as if he was repulsed. I squeezed his arm to reassure him, never had I seen him look this down or old.

'My son, I know your daughter is young, but if you want to protect your children and yourself, she is the only choice. The girl has to go into the evil forest to seal Ezyron for good. It's her destiny.' Madam Sarki informed my dad with finality.

Andrew who had been quiet finally spoke up a serious look on his face 'How long do we have before Ezyron rises and comes for us?' Madam Sarki stopped moving and her eyes became blank, it was like she left the room and only her body remained, it was creepy to watch, her mouth started speaking before her vacant eyes began to become animated again 'In five days' time. She needs to begin immediately.'

Andrew and I both looked at each other worriedly, five days was nothing and would be upon us sooner rather than later. I looked down at my dad, he was shorter than Andrew and I. We got the giant gene from our mum. He looked lost in thought, because whatever decision he came to it would be difficult for him. I think I could go on the quest, hopefully Andrew could go with me since he didn't have death hanging over his head.

'Daddy, I'm going to do it. I'll do it for me and you, I'll do it for our family.' If I made the decision for him, the guilt would be less on his heart and immediately I said so his shoulders dropped, like some of the weight on it had fallen off. He started crying again, but he also pulled me into a hug. 'Thank you Cupcake.' he whispered to me.

Andrew joined the hug also, and I felt something wet on my cheeks, that was when I realized I was also crying. After a short while we separated and Andrew was also crying, I think we both felt bad for dad and also didn't want to lose our only remaining parent to the evil that was Ezyron.

'She will go but not alone.' My dad said with no room for argument to Madam Sarki. 'Of course she'll need companions. Not even a mad person would send a child into the evil forest on her own. We'll start preparing tomorrow, so return with her.' Madam Sarki calmly said.

We settled into the long journey home in silence and bought food from the same fast food joint, my dad didn't like to admit it, but he was also not a fan of his wife's cooking. I had several missed calls from my friends and text messages asking if I was okay and hadn't been attacked at home, but I was too tired to tell each of them what had happened, so I just sent a broadcast message to them telling them I was fine and went out with my dad. By the time we got home it was past 10 p.m. and once we entered the building my step mum was waiting and raging.

'What is all this? You left the house this morning, you didn't say anything and see the time you're coming back! No call no anything!' She followed us as we moved from the entry of the house, 'We went to visit an old friend of their mother. Onye, it has been a long and tiring day, and we're tired, we just want to sleep, and not to stress you even more we bought food and have already eaten, let the children go to their rooms and let us go to ours.' Dad was trying to keep the peace and he knew the best way was to plead with her.

Andrew and I didn't waste time and left them behind as we went straight to our rooms, I took a quick shower and changed into my nightwear, laid on my bed and not long after I fell asleep. I was shocked when I woke up in the morning and did not have a single dream.

My friends arrived together a bit after 10 a.m. I was dressed and waiting for them in the living room, I had been alone and the channel was on Disney, but I was too distracted to focus as all I could think of was what Madam Sarki had said yesterday. I had made a group chat and asked if they could come over and they said they would.

'Hey guys,' I said and stepped aside for them to walk in.

I let them into my home and led them to the living room, once they were seated, Mara immediately asked me 'Hey, what happened? Why didn't you come to school yesterday? You were the talk of the day and everyone was waiting for you to show up.' Mara excitedly shared with me, I didn't know why she was excited, she knew how much I hated attention. More than anything I'm glad I missed school.

'I went somewhere with my dad, and the only reason I'm saying anything to you guys is because you're my best friends, so you've to promise to keep this a secret.'

They all eagerly promised as soon as I finished addressing them, but I turned my eyes on Maya and Nodebe, who were next to each other.

'Promise?' I asked again.

Nodebe and Mara looked at each other before confirming a second time. Mara talked too much when something excited her, and Nodebe could be a bit tricky when it came to keeping secrets. You could never tell how he would use a secret he knew against you. I had a captivated audience from start to finish as I narrated from how my dad reacted when I told him about the attack at the museum and meeting Madam Sakri and all she had said.

They were so entranced, when I finished speaking they didn't move as they were trying to warp their mind around what I had shared 'Guys?' I asked, snapping my fingers to get their attention. Slowly they came out of their shocked phase.

'Girl, that was the saddest yet most terrifying story I have ever heard,' Zoe said plainly.

The others nodded in agreement. I simply sighed. Why did I even bother? Now I looked more like a freak to my friends than ever.

'Annabelle what are we going to do? If what you say is true, the world will be in chaos in four days!' Mike said apprehensively and I had to try and reassure them. 'Ezyron was the cause of my horrible nightmares all this while and now it's threats and attempts at my life. Because I have a chance at sealing his tomb in the evil forest and he thinks I might succeed in sealing him forever, so he's determined more than ever to stop me. I'm going to do it.'

When I said I was going to go into the evil forest, their eyes widened but they didn't object.

'I think you should go-' Zina was saying when Mara interrupted him, I was a bit shocked because I had expected some objections about how insane and impossible it was, but Zina saying I should go stung. 'Zina, are you crazy? She could die!' I was happy Mara berated him with her response.

'I know that but if she doesn't, then the entire earth will be gone with us in it. Besides you didn't let me finish. I think you should go to save everyone but not alone. I'm coming with you.' Zina defended himself, looking at me with a small smile on his face. My heart was dancing in my chest and I shyly returned his smile.

'I'll also go, you need more than one person and I can fight.' Zoe piped in.

Nodebe and Mike counted themselves in and it was only Mara who hadn't made up her mind. Amongst all of us, she was the one who appeared the most visibly shaken. 'Look Mara, if you don't want to come, I completely understand.' I said reassuringly and smiled gently at her.

'No! I'm coming because you've always been there for me when I needed you. Now I want to be there for you, I just don't know how any of us will go without permission from our parents, since this is a life or death situation.'

It was true, even if they wanted to go, their parents would forbid it and have them banned from being friends with me.

'Look guys, you shouldn't have to worry about this. Some adults will accompany me and it would be alright, no need to get into trouble.' I said, sad because I would rather go with strangers and adults, than not have any friends when I came back.

'Actually Annabelle, I was serious when I said I would follow you.'

'Zoe, Really?' I asked surprised. 'Of course, Ezyron locked all of us with you, aside from Nodebe. We could have been released, but we were left with you, think about it, we're meant to go with you, right guys?' Zoe asked.

They all nodded their head, because Zoe was right, it wasn't by chance they had been trapped in that room with me.

'Ezyron may think you guys are also a threat because I was able to defeat his minions, with the help of you guys. So I really don't think you guys should risk your lives to go with me.'

'Stop. We're going with you, because I think we'll make a good team and also how much trouble can we get into for sneaking out and saving the world?' Mara confidently said, she was always trying to cheer me up.

'A whole lot,' Mike replied out of nowhere, and it had all of us laughing and relieving much of the tension that had taken hold of the room.

'Okay, we're doing this. We leave tonight, we don't have any more time to waste. My dad would drive us to my village, where we'll meet Madam Sarki who will tell us how to navigate the forest, before we set out on our quest are you ready?' I asked and their response was a affirmed 'Yes!'

'But don't we need weapons?' Mike asked a very smart question, I already had that covered of course, we couldn't fight if we didn't have tools. 'Leave that to me, my grandpa had a lot of hunting tools, my dad kept them, and will be giving them all to me for the quest.'

We all started talking about our fighting skills and how we always had to watch out for each other, when Mara started clapping excitedly and said 'Yes, this is exciting.'

This made all of us laugh, we were combating our fears by being positive and focusing on the action we would be dealing out. I was scared but I knew I had to be strong and trust myself and my friends. While lost in my thoughts a shadow on the plasma TV caught my attention.

Then a voice said 'You're going to be alone.' I knew it was in my head, and I was the only one who could have heard it. As soon as the voice stopped speaking the shadow disappeared. *I am not alone. Just come and try me!* I thought very loud and clear in my head, hoping whatever it was, was listening, because being with my friends made me more resolute about the fact, we could take anything down.

'No matter what happens, we'll leave tonight.' I reaffirmed

'To where?' The question came out of nowhere, loud and angry. We all looked toward the direction it came from and standing there glaring at us was my stepmother.

'Nowhere.' I finally answered her question.

'I just heard…' I interrupted her to say 'I was having a private conversation with my friends.' My tone was very hostile and she took offence 'Where are your manners? You spoilt brat!'

I ignored her and turned to my friends, who were already getting up to leave, not liking how my stepmother was behaving. I got up also and started apologizing for the interruption and the fact they were watching the maltreatment my stepmother was pouring my way.

'You and your brother are unbearable. Your mother gave birth to monsters!'

Her words hurt me to the core, how dare she? She never met my mother and knows nothing about her. I retaliated by screaming back at her 'Shut up! You witch! You know nothing about my mother!'

She slapped me hard across the face. My friends crowded around me protecting me from her, I was about to speak again, when Mara covered my mouth and she left us alone. I hate her and in this moment I hate my dad because how could he have ever fallen or married such an evil person.

My friends left not long after and I went and locked myself inside my room. Now that my anger had left me, I was embarrassed my friends had witnessed what had occurred and I hadn't done anything back to the witch. I laid on my bed staring at the ceiling, until my eyes got heavy and I slept off.

When I woke up, the sky was dark and I changed into fresh clothes and went downstairs to find my dad, so we could prepare and leave. I found him with the witch and he had on a serious look on his face.

'Hey Dad.'

'Hey Cupcake, what's up?'

'I'm ready when you are.'

I said in a coded manner, not wanting his wife to know what I was talking about. He looked at me sadly and shook his head. 'You're not going, I won't allow it.'

I was shocked, what had happened, I looked at his wife and she was smiling maliciously at me and I knew it was her fault and she had something to do with his change of mind.

'Why? How could you tell her? This has nothing to do with her. Do you now want me to die or you're ready to sacrifice yourself?'

I asked him bitterly, hating how weak he was and how reason

left him when it came to her, his evil witch of a wife. I watched my father's face pale, not expecting me to hurl the words that left my mouth at him, he was such a coward.

His wife scoffed and hissed at me, before speaking for her husband 'I'm his wife. He had to tell me and I forbid you, you're not going anywhere.'

'You can't forbid me from going anywhere. You have no authority over me.' I spat at her and she turned and looked at my father with shock, she contorted her face to that of one that was hurt by my words and my father, the sheep that he was immediately came to her defence.

'Annie, don't say that. She's your mother!'

My father that had never raised his voice at me, had the audacity to call someone who had been nothing but wicked to me since the day she arrived, my mother. She obviously had done something and bewitched him.

Tears started falling down my face and I looked at my father who had no look of remorse on his face 'She will never be my mother! She will never be my family, she is nothing to me.'

'Leave my presence this instant, you're grounded. You're an ungrateful girl, Annabelle and never speak to me about any mission again!'

I went to my room. Nobody would stop me from going on this mission, even my dad and I could not waste any more time.

My friends had lied to their parents they were going for a sleepover at Zoe's place, which was a good cover as Zoe's parent didn't pay much attention to what Zoe was up to and she could easily sneak out of her home. I informed them to come and get me by midnight because everyone but Andrew would be asleep.

We were going to kick Ezyron's butt.

I had skipped dinner and seized the opportunity to take the hunting tools from my dad's closet. Nobody had bothered with checking or calling me down for dinner, which was fine by me. Andrew, being the loving big brother that he was, brought me sandwiches he had personally made for me, not wanting me to starve.

I told him about what had occurred between dad and I and he was equally shocked and angry. He understood why I wanted to carry-on with my quest, and reluctantly accepted to stay behind when I explained the odd feeling of something not being with dad and someone needed to keep an eye on dad.

Since dad wasn't driving us again, we needed someone who could, so I turned to Andrew, who knew the perfect person. Mark, Mike's older brother. It took a lot of convincing and bribing on Andrew's path but Mark agreed and I had driving covered.

I got ready to leave, I wore clothes that would make it easy for me to move, yet still protect every inch of my skin. I emptied my backpack of my school things and filled it with mini bottles of water, chocolate bars and biscuits, as well as batteries for my torchlight, a power bank for my phone that could charge it fully 20 times before it died, after crosschecking I had everything I could possibly need, I carried the tools in my hands and I snuck out of the house to wait for my friends and Mark to arrive.

I thought I had escaped, but as I was about to open the gate and let myself out of the house, the voices of my dad's other family stopped me. I looked back to see the witch and her evil spawns approaching me.

'Didn't I forbid you from leaving this house?' She asked me and I rolled my eyes, wasn't she listening when I had first said it, she had no control over me. 'Nobody is stopping me, I don't want to die and I rather protect the world from evil.'

They all laughed like I had said something funny. 'I personally think you should go because there's no way you'll return alive. But Ezyron thinks you might succeed in sealing him.' Matt said, which confused me, how would he know what Ezyron thought?

'I will succeed and come back alive.' I spat my words confidently at them, and they glowered in return. 'We can't let that happen. We are his servants, we get a better life, when he's released, so we will stop you or anyone who seeks to destroy our happiness.' James said in an eerie and creepy voice.

They were Ezyron servants. It all made sense now. I needed to get out of here before they could harm me. I swiftly unlocked the gate and jumped out, banging the door close behind me and locking it from outside..

Right at that moment my friends arrived, which was perfect timing. They were wondering why I was panting and wanted to know what was after me, but I didn't have time to explain as I hurried them to get a move on, I started running with them on my heels so we could get out of the area.

By the time my gate opened it was too late for the witch and her children, who had now merged together to form a mutated red lion, with two hind legs and six forearms, six huge eyes and very large sabre teeth hanging from its mouth.

To our relieve, Mark was around the corner, he didn't ask any questions as we all piled into his car and he drove away from the scene, allowing us to put much needed distance from the lion.

Mike and Mark's mum was from Mbuzuo village, so Mark knew the way and I was just thankful he was willing to take us there no questions asked.

We thought we were in the clear, when we heard a loud roar, that almost had Mark swerving off the road, when he looked back, we were greeted by the sight of the demonic lion, which had grown bigger and was now glowing a bright red in the darkness. We needed to lose it and quick.

'Move!' I shouted, just as Zina asked 'Do you think you can lose it?' Mark shouted for us to use our seat belts and hang on tight, because his driving was about to become hazardous as he stepped on his accelerator and made a sharp turn to the right and a couple more turns, until the lion could no longer follow our trail.

'Um, Mark, where are you going? This is not the route. Are we lost?' I asked the panic in my voice, was very clear to whoever that was listening, but Mark reassured me 'Relax! This is another route I know. What is going on? Andrew didn't tell me, I would be dealing with the spiritual!' Mark questioned me, but he didn't take his eyes off the road. Mark's question, had everyone else looking at me, waiting for an explanation.

'That lion you saw, well that's my step-family.' I said calmly.

'I knew there was something fishy going on with your family, especially with how your stepmum has always treated you.' Zoe said.

'It all makes sense now, they are servants of Ezyron.'

'This means we have to be fast and seal Ezyron once and for all. Before they can harm your dad and brother.' Zina said with renewed energy. He was right, I hope Andrew could protect both himself and dad, because they obviously were going to turn to hurting them to get to me. The quicker we were, the sooner it would all be over.

Mark urged us to sleep, since we were all going to need all the energy we could before we started our quest. I was thankful for everyone that was with me right now and I prayed no harm came across any of us, because I couldn't imagine how I would react if harm came across any of my friends because of me.

I thanked Mark once again for agreeing to drive us there, and he had no qualms, saying he would always be there for Andrew, which meant he would also always be there for me and his brother Mike as well.

Before I slept, I used my phone to check on Andrew and gave him a rundown of all that had happened. He was shocked but wasn't surprised, he promised to be careful and stay with dad, until I returned.

Chapter 3

When I woke up, I felt strange and the reason instantly became clear to me, I had grown bigger. My head was touching the roof of the car and I had to slouch, so my neck wouldn't hurt. I greeted Mark who nodded his head at me but kept his focus on the road, the others were still asleep. Which was a good thing as they needed to rest up.

I didn't understand why I had grown but I hoped Madam Sarki would explain it too, even though now I had my doubts, what if Madam Sarki couldn't be trusted? Ezyron had to have someone working for him, to always keep tabs on me and most importantly what if I didn't win and I ended up dead as well as sentencing my friends to death along with me?

Mara's shriek drew me out of my thoughts. 'Annabelle, you… you…you…' she stammered, in shock. 'I also noticed. It is weird.' I agreed with her, so she would stop talking about it, as I already felt uncomfortable. The others stared waking up one after the other and of course the first thing they noticed was my height and their outcries of shock would have been hilarious if not for the fact it was at my expense and discomfort.

Once Mark got to the village, he had to ask me for directions to Madam Sarki's hut, which thankfully I knew because I had been paying attention when we left the other day with my dad.

'We're here kiddies,' he announced, as the car came to a stop once we were a few feet's away from Madam Sarki's hut. We all got down from the car, including Mark, who wanted to privately talk to his brother before he departed.

'Listen guys, this is your opportunity to leave now with Mark, no one will hold it against you if you changed your mind, because this is a dangerous—'

'Yeah, yeah, can we go? We've already made up our mind.' Zoe interrupted me. I ignored her and looked at everyone else, including Mike who had re-joined us. She could speak for herself, but not the others.

No one moved, I guess we were all going on an adventure together. We all thanked Mark and said our goodbyes. Mark wasn't leaving just yet, he wanted to sleep a bit in the car before he started the long journey back home.

I led them to the small hut that belonged to Madam Sarki and I knocked on the shut door. After a minute the door opened and Madam Sarki came out, clutching her wrapper over her chest. She looked older than she was some days ago and it seemed she was struggling to breathe, I wondered how she managed to remain on her feet. 'Good morning ma, please seat down o, you're not looking very well.' I said as I entered her hut and led her to a mat.

'He is getting stronger, my child. You must hurry.' Madam Sarki said weakly, she reached out for something and handed me an old and musty looking rolled up canvas, on it was a map. 'Ezyron is rising sooner than I thought, I think time is being manipulated, you must get to the forest and take four jewels from the different locations that I have marked for you on the map, this jewels will seal Ezyron forever.' Madam Sarki started coughing as soon as she finished speaking and she laid down.

'Go my child, you only have—'

'We have what? Ma?' I asked, I looked around to see if I could find her water to drink, when Nodebe got up in fear and exclaimed, while pointing at her legs 'Look!' I had forgotten the others were with me because of how quiet they had been, but I felt their presence as the horror unfolded before our eyes, she was disintegrating and quickly turning to sand before our eyes.

'Three days, my—' she couldn't finish speaking because her head as well as the rest of her was now sand.

'Ezyron did this, right?' Mara asked in fear, the question was rhetorical because we all knew the answer. I cleaned the tears that had fallen from my eyes and said a brief prayer for her before I ordered them 'Let's start moving,'

First, Ezyron took my mum, and then he took the life of an old lady who was trying to help me. The thought of my friends disappearing like that made me scared.

I couldn't let Ezyron take any more people, that had cared for me. I had to seal him forever. We consulted the map and decided we would head west first. As we walked it seemed like time was moving very fast, because it started to get dark faster than it usually did and I wasn't sure if the time was correct or Ezyron was playing games with time like Madam Sarki had said.

We all stuck close to each other but Zoe lagged behind a little and was oddly quiet, she was always talking or telling us one extravagant story or the other, something had to be bothering her and I wasn't so sure it was the journey we were on because she was the bravest amongst us. I wish she would speak or do something to relieve the tensed atmosphere we all were feeling.

'Hey, what's up? Are you alright?' I asked. Zoe looked at me and raised an eyebrow, curious about why I cared, but all she said was a plain 'Nothing.' I tried again, I wanted to engage her in a conversation but instead she lashed out at me 'Look Annabelle, I just want to be left alone.' I left her alone and moved onwards making sure we were on the right path.

People were finally talking to one another to pass time, when I randomly looked back and I saw Zoe and Zina whispering to one another, which instantly made me curious about what they were talking about, she obviously didn't want to talk to me, which didn't make sense.

After a while, I looked back again and saw Zina's hand was around Zoe's waist, they were wrapped close to one another as they walked and talked, happy smiles on their faces. I instantly became jealous. This was one of the reasons why I didn't really like Zoe. I always suspected she had a crush on Zina and that she has already won his heart since she was pretty.

We were surrounded by many tall trees, and Mara took over leadership as she was an excellent map reader, I sullenly stayed beside her.

'I'm tired,' Nodebe complained, I was also tired. It felt like we had been walking in circles for hours because all the trees looked the same, and nothing unusual had happened, I wondered why it was called the evil forest.

'Are you sure we're in the right place?' Zoe asked, speaking to no one in particular, so I didn't say anything. 'We're not lost.' Mara said, confirming by looking at the map again, I also took a look. We were on the right trail, but we had to find two trees, which were called 'The Forbidden Twins of Azyriona' It was useless because none of us would know what the trees would look like and the trees we were seeing all looked the same, which was very frustrating.

'Annabelle?' someone called out to me. It was Zina and for the first time in history, I didn't want to speak to him. 'Are you okay?' he asked as he came forward to stand beside me. I didn't look at him and briefly nodded, so he could leave me alone. 'You sure? Because you're being—'

'I'm fine, just frustrated,' I cut in coldly, seeing him with Zoe had made me bitter and jealous. Zina never got the chance to respond because Mike rushed up to us, I didn't know he had separated from the group, he looked pale and spooked, like he had seen something very terrifying.

'I think I found what we're looking for.' Mike shakily said, he pointed in a direction and we all started moving towards it, Mike didn't move as fast but it was clear he didn't want to be alone. I moved to him and put a hand on his shoulder to show my support.

Zoe's quick reflex saved us, as she lunged forward and firmly put her hands over Mara's mouth. Mike was right to be scared, my knees were shaking and all I wanted to do was run away, but I had to be brave, this was my quest more than the others and I had to be a leader.

Nodebe was hiding behind his big brother, shaking like a leaf as he said 'I don't have a good feeling about this.' Why had I let him come with us? He was just a baby, even though he acted very tough.

Everyone but Nodebe had been given a weapon for protection before we entered the forest, which he had loudly complained about, but we all refused because he was too small and dangerous with a weapon, because not only could he harm us, he could also harm himself.

Nodebe started complaining again, when Zoe threatened to get him captured and eaten by the wild animals in the forest. When Mara couldn't stand it anymore she said trying to diffuse the situation 'Zoe, calm down. He's just a kid,' but that further pushed Zoe and she became more enraged.

'So you defend the wrong now? What do you have against me, miss perfect?'

'Zoe, for real chillax.' Mike said holding her shoulder. 'Let go of me! Idiot!' Zoe said, pushing Mike to the ground. Soon, they were punching and hitting each other. The rest of us tried to stop them without getting physically involved, but it was no use.

Zina rushed in, trying to pull Zoe away; but Zoe's elbow hit his cheek, and I knew immediately it would have been very painful, his cheek was quickly turning into shades of red, but he didn't stop trying to separate Zoe and Mike. Mara, watched in fear, looking like she was about to break out in tears. Nodebe still angry with Zoe joined the fight to support Mike and was aimlessly hitting both Zina and Zoe.

It was pathetic and I was angry at their foolish display, this wasn't the time nor place for such behaviours and they were making so much noise, they would wake the tree man up. Nothing I said broke the fight, they were wasting time, until Mara screamed 'Stop!' it was very loud, because the scream resounded throughout the forest, she clapped her hands over her mouth, as we all turned to look at the tree, because we heard a disturbed groan from it.

'Who dares to make such noise while I sleep!' the tree bellowed before it opened its milky white eyes. It was so scary to watch my friends clutched each other, it finally noticed us, 'Impossible! How did you children get this far into the forest? If I was a deity you would all be dead, in fact no human would—' It stopped speaking once it eyes really took me in, his eyes narrowing as he stammered 'It is you …the water giant …'

'Who are you calling a water giant?'

I asked, fear surging my bravery. 'They kept it a secret from you? Yet they expect you to be their saviour? Ha! Ezyron was right! It would be so easy to eliminate you!' The tree said leaning forward. I put my hunting knife in front of me and saw that my friends had done the same with their weapons. 'Ho! I guess you're ready for battle. Unfortunately I can't move any part of my body due to that stupid curse of Azyriona. I don't know why that stupid witch, always interferes.' the tree grumbled.

'Where is the first jewel and how we going to get it?' Zina asked me he lowered his voice so that only I could hear him. Which made me remember there were supposed to be two trees, the second tree in question chose that moment to wake up as it let out a loud yawn, and a feminine voice questioned.

'What's going on Jisitu?'

'Baa, Chichi. It's of no concern of yours what is going on, let me be and go back to sleep, you nuisance.' Jisitu replied rudely, which infuriated Chichi who instantly said 'Oh Jisitu, you old pig. With that curse, you simply can't do anything—'

'Curse or no curse, you still don't have any power over me.'

'I didn't say such. What is done is done.'

'Oh shut up and stop trying to sound wise. I'm the wisest.'

'If you are the wisest, then stop being such a grouch and figure out a way to end this curse!'

Chichi exclaimed. Back and forth they went forgetting us and only focusing on themselves, their argument would have gone on forever if they clearly hadn't gotten on Zoe's nerves, she let out a frustrated scream. Chichi had been unaware of our presence and turned to look at us and gasped when she saw me.

'Is she…is she the one?' Chichi stammered, the fight had been drained out of her, since the moment she had spotted me. 'No o, she's the lumberman. Of course she's the one, your brain has always been slow.' Jisitu replied, but thankfully, Chichi ignored his obvious taunting, she learned forward and took a closer look at me.

'Stop don't come any closer!' I shouted in fear. 'Oh don't worry, I've been expecting you. We all have. Isn't that right, Jisitu?' she laughed after she asked her question and Jisitu replied 'Yeah, ready to roast her if that's what you mean.' and smacked his lips.

The hairs on my neck stood up and a shiver of fear went through my body.

'Not that, you fool!' Chichi said, which made Jisitu growl back 'Then what? You're backing out now?' Chichi smiled, her smile was scary because everything about it was evil, as if on cue, we all heard a growl in one of the trees.

'What was that?' Mara asked, her body visibly shook in fear.

'It's awake now, you children must smell very sweet. My servant! Come here and feast!' Chichi proudly bellowed, and we all heard a loud cawing sound, right before a gigantic bird swooped out of her right eye and landed in the space between the trees and us.

The contents of my stomach rushed up my oesophagus and I felt like puking, but I held it in.

Whatever the creature was, it was scary and frightening to look at.

Half of the bird had no feathers or skin to speak off, just its skeleton which was covered with a green mucus looking substance. Its two eyes were red and it had to be very hot because it was also releasing red smoke. We were watching each other, when it made the first move and spread out it wings and half ran and flew towards me, opening it's beak for me to see it had jagged and sharp teeth. I brandished my knife at it without even thinking, and it flew into a tree. 'She's getting stronger,' one of the trees said to the other in what was meant to be a whisper. 'Nice one, Annie!' Mara yelled from somewhere distant as the bird swooped down from high up ready to strike again.

Zoe began to shoot at it, despite some of the arrows lodging in its flesh, while some bounced off or missed it entirely 'It's not slowing down!' Zoe shouted as she kept on shooting, but she would soon be out of arrows.

Once the creature was close enough, Zina was the closest and struck it on its fleshy neck, but his cut didn't have that much impact because it was surface deep. The bird splayed its wings so it could strike at Zina, but luckily, he bounced away before it could hurt him.

Mike and I went for its sides and in sync we struck at the same time. The creature let out a loud screech and before our eyes engulfed in flames.

'Did we kill it?' Mike asked, panting.

The trees started laughing and Chichi answered Mike's question 'Don't feel too lucky. A creature of fire is quite hard to extinguish.' As we let the words sink in, we heard the loud cawing of the creature and we watched in horror as it appeared behind Nodebe and was heading for him. Nodebe was frozen in fear and couldn't protect himself because he had no weapon.

'No!' Zina and I screamed. Out of reflex I threw my knife with all my might, and it hit my target. My knife had struck one of its eye and was now stuck. The creature screeched in pain and retreated from Nodebe and took to a tree for cover.

I kept my eyes on the creature while the others ran to Nodebe, and once they were with him I ran for the creature, once I was close enough it started violently snapping at me. I jumped and grabbed a low branch which was within my reach, I launched myself up and grabbed the hilt of my knife, the moment I touched it I had a vision of *an eye*, but it was gone as quick as it came. I let go and landed on my feet with my knife. I shook my head to be sure I was still in the present.

The creature crashed to the ground, breaking most of its bones, yet still it was snapping at me. I didn't waste any more time and I smashed its head with my foot. With the creature dead before me, I looked down and saw something shiny in its chest. I bent down, hoping it was what I thought it was. It was a smooth and shiny ruby gem. I picked it up, not exactly thrilled about the fact that it was covered in green slime and I excitedly walked over to my friends with a big grin on my face, while the trees could do nothing but stare in shock, that they had been defeated.

'The jewel is ours!' I announced as I got close enough, and everyone released their bated breaths with relieve. I could see that Nodebe was fine, but as I came closer, their smiles vanished and were looking at me weirdly 'What's wrong? Is it the slime? Really guys?' I was about to reprimand them when Zoe said 'Your eyes.' She didn't take her eyes off my eyes and the others didn't also which was very worrying 'What's wrong with my eyes?' I asked, my fear hiking up.

'They're …They're—' Mara stammered.

'They're what?' I yelled, clearly annoyed with the suspense.

'They're white, Annabelle. Like you are blind.' Zina answered

Chapter 9

'I'm not blind. I can see everything as well as I could before.' I said, not believing them, even though I knew they were serious, maybe it was because I couldn't see them for myself. 'Your pupils are white, maybe it's part of the quest?' Mike said trying to reassure me and I was grateful.

'Here, see for yourself.' Zoe said, reaching into her back pocket she brought out a tiny mirror and threw it at me. I caught it and reluctantly looked into it and what I saw staring back at me left me shocked, but it quickly turned to anger and I crushed the mirror in my fist.

'Hey! That was mine.' Zoe shouted and glared at me, but I ignored her 'Why me? I'm rapidly becoming a giant and now my eyes! Why am I being turned into a freak?' I muttered to no one in particular.

I felt a hand land on my shoulder and turned to see Zina, looking at me with a gentle smile. 'The next task will give us an answer.' he said, trying to be reassuring. I returned his smile, but shook his hand off and turned my attention to the trees. I liked him yes, but I was still hurt and jealous, so I was still a bit irritational when it came to him.

The trees better had answers for me. I thought as I headed for them. 'Hey, Chichi and Jisitu!' I yelled, but there was no answer. Where their faces had been, there was nothing now. 'Their faces seem to have disappeared.' Mara said in a surprised voice. I looked closely at the trees, but something caught my attention, there was something in the trunk of one of the trees.

'There's something in one of them,' I said told them and turned to look at them but they were quite confused because they seemed to not be seeing what I was seeing.

'All I see is wood but—' Mike stopped midsentence and looked at me expectantly, Mike was so serious now, I would have loved it if he had said a joke, whether stupid or not, dry or not. I wanted the old Mike back.

'Look since you can see it, go and get it.' Zoe ordered, out of nowhere and it made me mad, who did she think she was? 'Don't order me.' I faced her, I towered over her and was glaring down at her, yet she didn't balk or back down. 'Then, I reckon you start moving if you want to be our saviour,' Zoe said, using a high-pitched voice to pronounce the last word. She was so annoying and my blood was boiling, but I couldn't let myself lose control.

I turned my back on them and walked towards the tree, to get what I had seen. It was Jisitu who I had to get the thing out of. Once I was closer, it was clear to me that my friends were right when they said all they could see was wood, I could see inside the tree, but the other part was covered in wood. I tried feeling the tree when my hand went through the bark like nothing was there.

I was so startled by what happened I started falling into the tree, but someone grabbed me and held on to me. I used the opportunity to grab the object, a dusty book and pushed myself out. I was assisted back onto my feet by whoever had caught me when I was falling and I turned to see it was Zina.

Why did it have to be him? Once they saw the coast was clear, the others came to join us.

'That was a bit close. Do you think all the trees do that?' Mara asked, looking at me, but I also didn't have an answer, my attention and gaze was fixed on the book.

'What's that?' Zoe asked, also staring at the book. 'Some book.' I said dusting off the cover with my hands. Written on the front cover of the book was the word PRISONOMIA, I tried opening it but it didn't budge.

'Well, open the book already.' Zoe snapped at me, as if she couldn't see I was struggling with the book. 'What does it look like I am doing? Admiring it?' I snapped back at her, tired of her behaviour . 'Just give it here.' Zoe responded and snatched the book from me. I watched in glee when her face started to turn as red as a tomato because the book refused to open.

I tried my best to hold in my laughter, but I couldn't and I wanted Zoe to feel dumb, so it was a win, especially when Nodebe started to laugh at her face and failure to open the book.

'Really just hand it over, so I can try, you look like a ticking bomb, that will soon go off.' Mike joked, which set off another round of laughter.

I was relieved Mike told a joke, which meant he was getting back to himself and it felt so good laughing at Zoe, she needed to be reminded she wasn't as tough or perfect as she was always claiming to be. Zoe's face turned sour and she roughly slammed the book on Mike's chest and sulked off.

It felt good for once, Zoe was on the receiving end of the merciless teasing, but my happiness was wiped clean when Zina left us to go and comfort her.

'Why is he always tending to her needs?' I thought but I didn't know it was aloud when Mara said 'Isn't that what boyfriends and girlfriends do?' I looked at Mara with alarmed eyes, I was in shock. 'They are… They're dating?' I asked, my hurt very apparent in my voice. 'Of course, since this term started. You didn't know?' Mara asked, not quite believing I didn't know.

I looked at Zoe and Zina. Zoe was now laughing and pinching Zina playfully and Zina retaliated by poking Zoe's nose. I felt like a complete idiot.

'Annie, it's okay if you didn't know. I didn't know at first but—'

'It's not that Mara,' I interrupted Mara. I wanted to tell Mara how I felt, but I didn't know how. Mara was about to speak once again when Mike let out a moan and we both turned towards him.

'This is so difficult. This is a brick, definitely not a book!' Mike proclaimed, I would have laughed, but I was too heartbroken after what I had just learnt.

'Can I hold it? It's not like I'm holding anything.' Nodebe asked Mike, who he was beside.

'Knock yourself out little dude, it's quite useless.' Mike said, tossing the book to Nodebe who excitedly caught it. I looked at the lovebirds and shouted harshly 'We need to get a move on. Time's ticking.'

I dug my hand into my pocket where I kept the ruby, wanting to feel it, but as soon as I held it in my hand, it started dissolving making me scream.

'What happened?' Mike asked, he had moved closer to me. 'The jewel—it just dissolved—dissolved in my hand.' I said shakily, and held up the hand in question to look at it, expecting it to also turn into dust, but nothing had happened to it.

'I think, it will come back when you need it.' Mara said and I nodded at her, hoping she was right because there was nothing else I could do but to carry on with our journey.

I pulled out the map from my backpack, where I had safely tucked it when I had seen the trees. The map had some mysterious power, because there was a huge X mark on the location we were at, knowing we had gotten the first gem.

'This way!' I said and looked at everyone, who had gathered around. My eyes caught that of Zina, and we held each other's stare longer than necessary, before he smiled at me, I rolled my eyes and handed the map to Mara, so she could navigate and we could both lead the way.

I felt betrayed by Zoe, but really what would I expect from her? She had always been obnoxious and selfish. I never told Zina I liked him and he didn't owe me anything and could be with whoever he wanted to be with, so really Zina and I just weren't meant to be.

Nodebe let out terrified scream and we all froze and instantly drew our weapons, ready to come to his aid. Nodebe was frozen, his eyes were scared, in his arms was the book, but instead of it being shut tight, it was open and a huge scaly arm with sharp pointy talons attached to a claw came out of the book. A terrifying screech came out of the book and whatever it was would have come out if I did not get to Nodebe in time and shut the book with his hands. The arm immediately got sucked back into the book which fell from Nodebe's hands, as Nodebe started shaking and tears started streaming down from his eyes.

'Jesus, what was that?' Mara asked shakily. I turned to look at the rest but they were still stunned. A question bothering me, but Zina beat me to it. 'How could you open the book but we couldn't?' Zina asked his brother, but Nodebe didn't answer, and I looked at him.

His head was now down and he was staring at the book at his feet. I put my hand on his shoulder, but he still didn't move.

'Hey Nodebe, do you mind telling us—' I couldn't finish my sentence because Nodebe looked up at me at that moment and I scrambled away as I yelled out in fear.

His eye balls were shimmering gold and his face had lost its colour. Nodebe reached out and grabbed my hand, his grip was too strong for that of a nine years old and spoke.

'Time doesn't seem to be on your side and my time to feed is nearing so fast. And you've found the perfect souls to fill me.'

As soon as Nodebe stopped speaking he blinked furiously and the colour started to return to his face, although his eyes were still gold, he was coming to and looked confused. Once he released me I moved back and away from him.

Zina moved past me and crouched down in front of his brother and asked him 'Noddy? What happened?' But Nodebe was confused and didn't know whatever it was that had possessed him. I looked up at the sky and saw that Nodebe or whoever it was, was right. If we didn't move faster the sky would become completely dark.

'We need to keep moving!' I shouted, walking fast to the front to join Mara once again, I looked back to see Zina was looking at me, expecting me to explain to him what had just happened. I wasn't going to so I looked away and began to move and everyone else fell in line behind us. My mind couldn't stop replaying Nodebe words, when Mara paused and gave me the map, and when I saw we were close to our next destination, I froze.

'Annabelle, what's wrong?' Mara asked me and I turned to face her and address the others, already exhausted by what was to come 'Get ready, I think we're about to meet our worst nightmare.'

Chapter 5

'Our worst night—worst nightmare?' Mara always stammered when she was scared, freezing as she imagined her worst nightmare. 'Can we stop here? I'm not sure if I want to meet my nightmare.' Mara said quickly.

'Come on Mara, I know you're scared but—' I was consoling her when Zoe abruptly said cutting me off as usual 'For crying out loud, just grow up!' which did no good and only frightened Mara some more, so I continued reassuring her 'We all need to stick together, if we want to make it out of here alive and just trust your guts and be courageous.'

'We would rest after the second task, we need to rest and recharge to functioning properly.' Zina added in, but Zoe wanted to have the last word and said 'Instead of chatting, why don't we move because while we're standing here wasting time, a deity is rising.' I rolled my eyes and we continued moving.

'Ouch!' Mara cried out after a while, she had fallen.

'Mara, what happened?' I asked and crouched down to check on her while the others were hurried up from behind us.

'My foot hurts. I think I hit a stone,' she said rubbing her foot and wiped at her face. 'That's it? Mara, you made us stop for—' Zoe was about to finish when a screech interrupted her.

'What was that?' Nodebe asked, I looked at him to see his eyes were still golden, but he seemed to be fine and his senses had been returned to him. I was about to ask him if he felt alright or was feeling strange, when Mike asked 'What's that?' and crouched down beside Mara and picked up a huge lump of molten crystal with his two hands. It was unusual and shouldn't have been lying out on the ground here just like that and we all assumed it was what had made Mara trip.

'It looks like—'

Before I could finish, the loud and terrible screech sounded out again, which made everyone clutch at their ears, trying to block out the sound and Zoe shouted, while holding her ears 'What is that? It hurts!' The sound was terrible but it wasn't affecting me as bad as it seemed to be affecting them because I wasn't covering my ears.

It happened so fast, Zoe didn't have any time to protect herself. An eagle like bird made out of stormy clouds swooped down from the sky and used it's big claw to lift Zoe up by her shoulders and was lifting her high up in the air and all she could do was scream.

'Zoe!' Zina shouted, looking up in fear at the eagle which was flying away with Zoe. Zina looked at me with fear and worry in his brown eyes. 'Annabelle, what was that? Why didn't you do anything!' he asked accusingly and I was at a loss for words. I was equally in shock, but if I was being honest, I was glad it took Zoe and if it was up to me I would have marked her off as dead, but Zina and the others would not let me and would also think I was a monster.

But I really couldn't, because even though she was annoying and condescending, she didn't have to go with me and I owed it to her to save her. I really hated how I had to be the hero.

'All right, whatever that thing was, was in the form of a bird so we just need to find it's nest, once we do that, we'll ambush it at all corners and free Zoe, hopefully we get to her before it's too late.' I announced solemnly and we all agreed, we had to find the tallest tree so we consulted the map and luckily enough, the tallest tree was on the path we were currently on.

Maybe I was actually born to be a leader, because I had successfully motivated and increased our morale, we were already heading towards the tree when Mike called out to me and stopping everyone.

'How about we keep this baby?' Mike asked holding the crystal rock like it was a trophy. 'Mike, we don't have time for such games.' Mara said, crossing her arms over her chest, she had a little limp to her walk but apart from that she seemed fine.

'But we'll be rich; this thing would cost a fortune. Please Annie.' Mike pleaded and took on puppy eyes, which made me laugh. Mike always had to have his way because if he didn't all hell would break loose. He and Zoe had that in common, but Mike was much more reasonable.

'Fine!' I said and he handed the crystal to me, for safe keeping in my backpack. 'No more time wasting, before Zoe becomes demonic bird food.' my words seem to take the glee out of Mike and he instantly became serious as we all walked as fast as we could towards the tallest tree, which was the direction the bird flew to.

After what felt like an hour, I spotted the weird stormy bird resting high up in a nest, it's wings tucked and it's eyes closed. I motioned for everyone to be quiet with my hands and took cover behind a tree. 'Where's Zoe?' Zina whispered into my ear and I pushed him back a bit, as I scanned the area, when my eyes landed on a sack made up of a yellow like substance, which looked to be holding something that had a human shape, hanging from a tree branch a bit lower than the nest, the substance kept swinging and shaking like whatever was inside it was struggling. I guessed Zoe would be the thing trapped inside it and was about to inform the others of my assumption, but they had all followed my gaze, because all their faces were scrunched up in disgust.

'Please, tell me Zoe isn't there?' Mike said with a scrunched up face. 'Come on, this is our chance.' I said and was about to move when someone tugged at my shirt. I turned around to see Nodebe, holding my shirt and looking upwards. 'Nodebe, we don't have time for—'

'Shhh!' Nodebe said, shutting me up before I could finish. 'Nodebe, that ant—'

'Wait, listen!' Nodebe said his eyes becoming blank, like he wasn't with us anymore and he was starting to scare me when, his eyes became animated again and said to all of us 'Get down!' we didn't hesitate or question him and we all laid on the floor.

Another birdlike creature swooped down and landed before the tree where the other was nesting. But this one had some human features, had a feminine body, which was orange in colour, with wings for hands and claws for feet. It had black slits for eyes as well as slots for nose. It had pink lips and its hair looked like a nest. I looked at my friends and they were equally stunned.

'Is that—' Zina was about to finish when Nodebe interrupted him 'Annie,' he started and stopped when we all looked at him. 'What?' Mike asked, holding his head with a confused expression.

'Animate.' he stated, then further explained 'Animate, it's what the book says.' he held the book out to us.

'You opened it again?' Mara asked, her hands going to her waist as she looked down at him with disapproval 'I had to, I know how to use it.' Nodebe in a tone that said no argument.

I let out a sigh and ran my fingers through my hair. 'Okay, so what does it say?' there was no choice, we didn't have a clue what we were doing and if we had a small advantage we had to use it.

Nodebe quickly opened the book stopped on a page with 'ANIMATE' written in bold letters at the top. There was a picture beside the writing but the picture was not of the bird. 'That isn't the bird.' I said stating the obvious, but the others agree with me.

'Exactly because that isn't its real form. It's just an aspect, a part of him or her.' Nodebe tried to explain.

'Him or her?' I asked.

Nodebe nodded his head and began to read the passage.

ANIMATE

Many legends claim that this group of individuals called Animate were divergent due to their reincarnations into different animals. Osmarue, the god of living beings created them as a gift to his wife, Osmirin, goddess of the Edomma River who had tricked him into giving her this gift, because she wanted slaves serving her. She later tricked her husband into entering the mouth of a forbidden beast with the help of Odaise, his elder brother who was also her lover. But that wasn't the end of Osmarue, as he reincarnated in one of the Animate, and together with the others they took down and buried Osminin and Odaise in the forbidden Abyss alive. The Animate had roam freely on land, water and air after that, until a mysterious storm came and took them away. Ever since there has been no trace of their existence.

After Nodebe finished reading, he looked up to see our confused faces. The names did not make any sense to me but they sounded familiar.

'But if they don't exist again, why is—' I was interrupted by the wind, which was picking up its pace and everywhere was suddenly getting dusty.

'Look—Annie.' Mara said, and I looked up to see what she was looking at. The wind had picked up, and the sand and dust around it had formed a tornado. It was so harsh and strong that I had to shield my eyes with my hands.

But as quick as it had started the wind stopped howling and when I opened my eyes, everything was back to normal and the sand and dust had settled. The Animate had changed her form and was now a girl with orange hair and skin colour as golden as the sun. She was small in stature and was dressed in a tube top and a short wrapper tied around her waist. As she walked on bare footed, her multi-coloured eyes seemed to roam around looking for something.

'Rariri, where's food?' she asked looking up at the huge bird which had been sleeping.

'*O no eba*,' the bird said sluggishly.

I looked at my friends, and Mara mouthed, 'It can speak in Igbo?' I shrugged and went back to paying attention to the Animate. She looked towards the direction where Zoe was kept and smiled. She walked briskly towards the yellow substance, and her nails transformed into claws, which she sunk into the substance and began to rip the thing apart.

'Is she going to eat her now?' Mara asked me in disbelief. 'We are going to strike now.' Mike said to Zina, who nodded in agreement. They took off before I could tell them to be careful, they weren't dealing with a human, even if she looked like one.

I watched her face change from confusion to surprise and finally settled on anger. She focused on the boys, and opened her mouth and a pair of fangs that were like that of a sabre-toothed tiger rapidly grew, she hunched her back and growled ready for the battle.

Zina struck first, but the Animate was faster and moved stealthy, so she easily dodged the hit. She snarled at him in annoyance, before she jumped up in the air, arms outstretched as if she intended to slice him open when she landed on him. Zina would have been badly injured or worse bleeding to death if Mike hadn't moved quickly and raised his weapon to attack her from behind, but they were no match for her, as she sensed the hit was about to come and swung around mid-jump, grabbed the weapon Mike was holding on to and swung it and Mike along towards Zina, which sent both of them crashing to the floor.

'Eat!' she screeched, as she walked towards them, I wasn't going to let her eat my friends and we had to do something, so I gave up my cover and swung my knife at her, but her senses must have been heightened because she knew it was coming and moved away just in time for it to hit a tree and remain on it.

'This was a bad idea,' Mara muttered and began to bite her fingernails as she started shaking also, while Nodebe didn't seem to be scared, I took a deep breath and picked up my shattered pieces of courage and put it back together.

'It's now or never!' I said.

I jumped out of my hiding spot and ran at full speed to cut her off, she turned around to face me, when I swung myself at her, we ended up tumbling over each other and by the time we stopped, I was on top of her, my head spinning. At first, she narrowed her eyes squinting at my face, and when she finally took my face in clearly, her multi-coloured eyes widened in fear and she seemed to shrink.

'Stay away from my friends.' I warned, pinning her down.

'Mercy! Geantoa! Mercy! Won't do it again…won't do it again!' she cried as her lips began to quiver. It was shocking, I wasn't expecting her to cower because of me, when she had been nothing but vicious from the moment she had arrived.

'What did she just call you?' Zina asked with a confused look, they had all gathered around me now, holding their weapons ready to strike just in case she tried to harm me.

'Geantoa, Geantoa, no, no!' She continued to cry out while I still had her pinned to the floor, but she wasn't trying to escape, she was cowering.

'I don't know—' I was interrupted by the muffled screaming from Zoe, who was still stuck and dangling in the tree.

'Zoe!' Zina shouted, after we had all forgotten about her momentarily. Mike and Zina climbed up the tree to the branch she was hanging on and carefully Zina went forward and tried to slice the substance open, it easily gave way. Zina pulled Zoe out with the help of Mike, and they brought her down from the tree.

Once they were on the ground, and she knew she was safe again, she finally took in her appearance, which was yucky. She was covered in saliva, and she was about to blow out on us, which Zina quickly tried to diffuse.

'Zoe calm down, it's—'

'Calm down? I'm covered in giant bird's mucus. Is that normal?' Zoe yelled back at Zina.

I returned my attention to the creature I had pinned to the ground and tried to scare her into speaking 'Okay, start talking or I, the…um…Geantoa, will cut your…tongue off.' I firmly said and the forest became eerily quiet, even my friends had stop bickering and giggling.

'Cut your tongue off?' Zoe asked with narrowed eyes at me, her red hair was now matted to her face, no thanks to the mucus. I shrugged in response because she didn't know what had happened and she was once again trying to undermine me.

'Tell me who you are and why you are eating people' I said, and I noticed something odd, she had shrunk in size under my hands.

'My name is Kiola and I am an Animate, a descendant of Osmiyire, the chief priest of Osmarue. The bird there is my mother, Eswena Rariri who was cursed by Epitoh, the daughter of the deity, Ezyron, to stay in this form until her last breath. I took your friend out of hunger. We need the food and we were trying to avoid predators. In this forest, the motto is kill or get killed.' Kiola said, staring at me with sincerity in her eyes, her gaze was very intense, but I was reeling from the bomb she had just dropped, Ezyron had a daughter and that was very worrying.

'Is Ezyron's daughter still alive?' Mike asked, his hold on his hunting knife tightening. 'Unfortunately yes. Ezyron may soon rise, and she will stop at nothing to free him. But if the prophecy is true, maybe you can save us.' Kiola said to like I would know the prophecy she was talking about.

Before I could ask her about the prophecy I noticed it was already dark and would be darker soon. We couldn't waste any more time if we wanted to retrieve the second jewel today.

'Oh goodness! Time is running out. We need to get to the Cave of Fears now!' I said to my friends, as I got up and dragged Kiola up with me, I noticed she had perked up when I had said the Cave of Fears.

'No, the Cave of Fear is dangerous. People die. Geantoa might not, but they will.' she said and pointed in the direction of my friends.

A scream escaped from Mara's lips and she clamped a hand over it instantly. I glared at Kiola who dropped her finger and looked chastised. 'Kiola, we know what we signed up for. Tell your mother and whoever that is like you people, to stay clear of us and leave us alone. Understand?'

'Please, I want to help—if Geantoa allows. I want to help. I want to be on Geantoa's good side. Please, mercy.' Kiola begged, I was wary to let her come with us, especially as I didn't understand what Geantoa meant, but if we had someone with her abilities with us, we had a higher chance of succeeding.

'Fine but you will stay by my side and not attack any of the people that are with us.' I informed and reminded her, because she was only afraid of me and the others could barely harm her, Kiola instantly became happy and nodded her head enthusiastically in understanding.

I felt self-conscious, because it felt like someone was watching me, but when I looked around, I didn't see anything, so I shrugged it off.

'Let's leave before my mother wakes up. She won't mind fighting a Geantoa for her meal.' Kiola said and motion for us to get going so I started walking away with her on one side and Mara on the other side of me.

Chapter 6

'There it is!'

Kiola announced when a huge opening on a rocky mountain came into view, even from where I was I could tell the inside of the cave would be very dark. We increased our steps and I brought out my torchlight, because it had gotten somewhat darker and our path needed to be illuminated. The closer we got to the cave, the colder it got and what was shocking was how quick it was becoming cold.

'Why is it cold all of a sudden? It's not even meant to be this cold anywhere in Nigeria' Mara complained, wrapping her arms around herself and rubbing her sides, trying to warm herself up.

'This is bad. Otimesa is here.' Kiola said, pausing and moving backward in fear 'Who is that?' Mike asked, he couldn't mask his fear and he also had moved backwards. 'The fear catcher. This is her lair, she uses people's fear to defeat them and absorb their souls.'

'Why?' I asked, knowing Kiola would have an answer 'She was imprisoned by her master, Rukewiwe, the deity of lost souls. She tried to kill Rukewiwe by luring the diety into the mouth of the underground, Babu. She failed and was punished for eternity.'

'All we have to do is avoid an evil fear creating witch and retrieve the jewel from the cave? I think we've got this.' Zoe said, removing the dried substance that was now sticking on all over her body and hair.

'We should get moving now. It's not safe to be moving around in the forest when it's dark, and I doubt that we will reach our destination, wherever it is today.' Kiola mumbled, forgetting her fear and led the way.

I had not told Kiola about our mission to stop Ezyron, what if that was the prophecy she had been speaking about. Nodebe tugged me and I realized I hadn't moved with the others, and I fell in step with him.

Kiola stopped walking, bent down to pick up tree branches, I watched her open her mouth and breathe fire unto them one after the other, handing them to everyone. I turned off my battery powered torch and put it in my backpack.

We entered the tunnel and the wall immediately caught my attention, craved onto it were strange symbols, which at first, I couldn't understand and looked like gibberish, but the more I looked at them, the clearer it became and I could read and understand them.

Eyes that look beyond
One from the four foundations

I was about to read the next line when Mara called out to me, so we could get a move on and get out of the cave before it got too late. 'What were you looking at?' Zina asked as soon as I joined them 'Some symbols on the wall, not so important.' I replied, even though I had dismissed it, I still felt that it was important, but there was no need worrying the others.

'Otimesa is here, if there are symbols on the wall.' Kiola whispered, which sounded even scarier because we all had gone quiet and I felt like my heart was in my throat. I gulped and beckoned the others to keep on moving, because I could see from their faces they were also wary and scared.

The farther we walked into the cave the colder it became, but the fire on our torches didn't go out. We were all walking with Kiola leading when a high-pitched scream broke our silence.

'Mara!' I shouted, my heart beating fast in fear, I spun around to see her screaming and fighting with nothing. She looked crazy, yet she wouldn't stop screaming and crying, something was obviously attacking her even though I couldn't see it. I was moving to calm her down, when she stepped backwards and fell into a small puddle, still screaming.

I looked at the others, who were frozen and watching her in confusion but none of them were moving towards her to aid her, when I reached her and tried to help her up, she screamed at my touch, still blinded by her fear and recoiled away from me.

'Mara! It's me Annabelle! What's wrong Mara? Mara?'

'They're everywhere!' she sobbed, still cowering and fighting off whatever it was that was making her afraid. 'What are you—' before I could finish me sentence, I saw what was attacking her, it was a group of zombies and they were trying their best to get a piece of Mara.

I went into action immediately I swiped at the nearest zombies with my hunting knife, which easily went through them and they burst into nothing. 'Uhm guys, a little help?' I called over to them, especially Kiola, she would be able to take down all the zombies without breaking a sweat.

'We can't see anything. We don't know what you're fighting.'

Mike helpfully supplied. I was about to tell Kiola to come and help me, when she spoke up 'The Geantoa must be seeing the girl's fear. We aren't meant to see each other's fear, that is why we can't help.'

'What?'

I turned around to look at Kiola, and that was all the zombies needed because immediately my focus wasn't on them they grabbed Mara and started dragging her off, no matter how hard I tried to pull her back the zombies were stronger and they disappeared with her.

'Mara!' Zina exclaimed in fear, all their eyes were widened, because from their point of view, Mara had been dragged away by nothing.

'Where was she taken?' Zoe asked me 'How do you expect me to know!' I replied, my voice raised out of frustration.

'One down. Six more left.' Kiola randomly said and why was she here if she couldn't even be useful. I looked at my scared friends, wondering which of us would be next, when Nodebe let out a deafening scream.

Something was burrowing its way out from the ground and when the hole was wide enough the cute face of a cat popped up, which didn't make sense, cats didn't dwell below the ground. Nodebe was afraid of cats, and he was completely terrified and even I became scared when it fully came out, the cat's head was attached to the body of a snake, and at the other end of it was another cat's head.

The monster raised their head up and formed an upright U with their body, while hissing at Nodebe, who didn't stay still and ran for cover heading for his older brother. I ran for the monster and sliced one of its head off and it quickly dissolved but grew back almost instantly. The monster became angry and opened its mouths I ducked just in time as they released a deadly blast of fire in my direction. The time it took me to dodge was all the monster need and it was slowly wrapping itself around Nodebe. Nodebe was screaming and crying, his screaming was horrifying to hear, because his fear and terror was loud and heart-breaking to watch.

I watched in horror when the monster somehow started dragging Nodebe away, We all tried going after him, but something was holding us back, stopping us from moving.

'Two down. five more to go.' Kiola said and I turned to face her. 'You're not being helpful, we all can see what is happening!' I shouted at her in anger and she cowered in fear. I didn't want to lose my friends, it was horrifying how their fears were being used against them.

'Kiola, what will happen to Mara and Nodebe?' I asked, Kiola hesitated at first, still wary after I had shouted at her, she meekly answered me 'I'm sorry, Geantoa but—' Kiola stopped speaking, when Mike let out a deafening scream.

Mike was gagging, he was struggling for air, and couldn't breathe, immediately I saw why, Mike was drowning. The space around him was filled with water. Mike's fear was, drowning. I ran to where Mike was choking and entered the water and grabbed him, but I didn't know how I was going to drag him out, because where ever I pulled him, the water followed and the force of the water was getting stronger and it was harder to pull him, Mike passed out, and immediately a whirlpool surrounded Mike and he and the water were gone.

I could breathe underwater, that realization shocked me. I turned to face Zoe and Zina, who had tears streaming down their faces, were looking around as if waiting for whatever to pop out and grab them, when I realized Kiola was nowhere to be found.

'Where did Kiola go?' I asked them, which made them aware of the fact that Kiola had deserted us.

'She was here, a minute ago,' Zina quietly said, sniffling. Zoe remained quiet, and we both became tensed when we heard someone say her name.

Zoe and I turned towards the direction the voice came from, and I felt Zoe go numb instantly. The owner of the voice was a girl about six years old with long red hair, wearing a white dress. The girl's face was pale and she has green and blue veins intertwined on her solemn face. When I looked closer, I realised that the girl looked like a mini Zoe.

Maybe it was Zoe when she was younger? 'Zoe.' the little girl whispered as she narrowed her different coloured eyes at Zoe, I looked back at Zoe and she was shivering and freely crying. 'No. No. No! I didn't mean to, I swear.' Zoe said, scrambling backwards and away.

'You did this, you killed me.' the small girl said, still moving towards Zoe's direction.

'I swear, you have to under—'

Before Zoe could finish, the girl let out an awful sounding scream and shouted 'LIES!' I watched the little girl multiple from one into five and so it continued, all of them chanting 'LIES!' and marching towards Zoe, I knew there was no point attacking them because they wouldn't just reintegrate and be undeterred. I watched helpless as they rounded upon her and dragged her away.

Zina looked helpless and remained on the floor, he had given up, no hope was left and I guess he was waiting for his fear to capture him too. I went to him and put my hand on his shoulder in solidarity. I didn't want to see Zina's fear, I felt like I would be invading some kind of privacy.

'I'll find a way to fix this and get everyone back.' I vowed to him, but Zina didn't respond or acknowledge me, he was so lost in his thoughts, when he finally looked at me, I saw he had started to sweat and I knew his fear had come and was behind me.

I turned to look at what had come to take him away, and I dropped my knife because staring back at us was another me.

Chapter 7

How was it that I was Zina's biggest fear? I stared at my clone; she was dressed just as I was and the startling thing to see was the white eyes, I really looked strange with it. I looked at Zina who cowered when I returned my gaze to him.

'Zina.' I called, searching his face for an explanation, why would he be afraid of me? My clone started speaking to him also 'Zina, it is time to tell her.' Tell me what? I looked at Zina, who was refusing to look at me or my clone. 'What is she talking about?' I asked.

'I don't know.' Zina said, refusing to look at me, I watched my clone approach Zina, her lips shaped in the form of a smirk. 'Come on, Zina. You knew it would happen.' Quick as lightning she grabbed the front of Zina's shirt and pulled him up to face her. 'You know what she's capable of. You saw it.' my clone said.

'Zina, what is she talking about?' I asked, I couldn't think of why he would be scared of me and the suspense was frustrating me, the more upset I was, the world became smaller and I knew I had grown again.

'The sword you gave me. It can see into the nearest future, and I have a good guess what Geantoa means.' Zina said remorsefully, I blinked and the world shrunk again, I had grown even taller. 'Why didn't you say anything before Zina!'

'I wasn't sure. I wanted to help, to be sure that maybe it was a curse that we could—'

'And what if it is really what I am? Does that mean our friendship will end?'

'Annabelle, I didn't say that. I just want to help.'

'How have you helped?'

My clone repeated what I had said, but her voice had a resounding echo, I turned around and saw more clones of me where surround us.

'You knew I was different, the first day we met. You were only nice to me because others teased me, and you felt that it would make you look good not because you're good!' My clones said in unison.

'Annabelle, please don't believe them. It's not true.' Zina said desperately. 'Liar!' The first clone shouted and struck the ground with her huge fist, the ground broke apart. Their eyes turned blue and started to glow as they stampeded towards Zina. Even though Zina had confused me and was keeping secrets from me, I still had to defend him. I slammed into one of my clones and stuck her in the chest, and I also felt the pain on my chest, I staggered backwards and tripped over another clone, which had me fallen backward and kicking another clone in the face, which made my own face start aching, and it was very painful, I took a few seconds to recover, but it was too late, my clones along with Zina were gone.

I had been walking for ages and it felt like I was walking in circles, yet nothing came out for me. I had returned back to a moderate size and wasn't a giant anymore, and I kept replaying all that had happened especially when Zina had been taken. Why wasn't I being attacked by my fear? I was feeling so weak and tired, when I leaned against the wall of the cave to rest for a minute, it wasn't up to a second later when a thunderous voice boomed across the cave.

'Annabelle Nguma, we meet at last.'

It couldn't be who I thought it was, yet I had to ask 'Ezyron?'

'Child you're smart, but foolish to have really believed you could stop me. You're weak. A pathetic mere human. You rely on and depend on too many things and never yourself.'

Ezyron said in an eerie voice before letting out an evil laugh, I couldn't see the deity, when I saw someone coming out of the shadows. It was Mara.

'Mara!' I shouted and ran to hug her, and ask her how she had escaped but she remained stiff. When I let go, I knew why. Her glasses were missing and her pupils were glowing red and her outfit had changed, her hair was loose, she was wearing brown native attire with beads engraved onto the neckline and it was a really short dress, which was unlike Mara.

'Mara?'

'Mara is gone Annabelle. How dumb can you be not to realise that?' Mara's mouth was moving but it wasn't her speaking, the voice didn't belong her. Ezyron was speaking through her.

The rest of my friends came out of the shadows and were dressed in the same attire Mara was wearing, only the guys had on trousers.

'What did you do to them?' I shouted at nothing 'Only creating your worst nightmare. Finish her!' Ezyron ordered, and the things that looked like my friends charged at me.

Zoe slammed into me and rolled away to shoot an arrow at my head, which I dodged and retaliated by using the butt of my knife to slam the side of her head. Another arrow narrowly missed my ear, and I turned around to see that it was Mara, who was aiming another at me was ready to fire again. I threw myself at her, laying low and I was able to knock her down for the time being.

I was getting back on my feet when I heard a deadly growl and I looked around to see a large dog with red smoking eyes watching me like I was its prey.

'Nice doggie' I said calmly, trying to get my fear under control, but I wasn't fast enough as it let out an angry bark. It moved and snapped it jaw at me hard, but I moved in time, if not whatever part of my body that it would have capture would have been ripped off.

I saw Nodebe had the mysterious book I had taken from Jisitu open and he had on a smile, that was pure evil, he closed the book and I realized where the dog had come from. That book shouldn't have been in his hand or in the presence of Ezyron, I was going to get it from him, when I was hit from both sides and I went crashing to the floor clutching my sides, groaning with pain, I looked up to see Zina and Mike were my attackers, they had kicked my ribs from both sides and they had their swords raised ready to strike down on me, I was stunned that my friends could easily be brainwashed to attack me, but I wasn't going to go down without a fight. With all my might I raised my feet up and kicked them away from me.

Mara choose that moment to pounce on me again and struck me in the shoulder with an arrow. The pain was so intense, I let out of scream, but that was cut off when Mara kicked me in the face twice. Zoe came to join her and I felt a stabbing pain in my leg, as another arrow pierced through my skin. I was bleeding out and getting fuzzy in the head, due to how much pain I was feeling and blood I was losing.

I began losing consciousness, my eyesight became blurry and I could only make out figures towering over me. 'It's over, Annabelle.

The game is over!' Ezyron's voice echoed in my ears and was the last thing I heard before I was engulfed in darkness.

The smell of fire choked me a bit, but I was glad I could smell. At least I knew I had survived. I opened one eye trying to observe my surrounding, and saw that the cave seemed wider and spacious. I opened my second eye, expecting to see myself in chains, but instead found myself wrapped in a blanket. There was a fire by my left, and I tried to sit up, but the pain in my shoulder told me otherwise.

I came through, because of the strong smell of burning wood. I opened my eyes and it took me awhile to adjust to the dimly lit space. I was in some sort of cave, which immediately had me remembering my last moment before I had fainted, and explained why my body felt badly bruised and battered.

I sat up my heart in my throat, it was hard because of the sharp pains moving caused on the part of my shoulder that had been pierce. But what made me hyperaware was I wasn't in chains, I seemed to be on my own and I was even covered with a woolly blanket. Whoever had seen to me or rescued me had cared enough about my comfort. So I was sure it wasn't Ezyron who had captured me.

I heard footsteps approaching and I dropped back down and closed my eyes, pretending I was still asleep. Whoever it was came to my side and I felt a rough palm on my forehead, like the person was checking my temperature.

Whatever or whomever that had rescued me sat down beside me and took hold of me, I was frightened but I didn't want to give myself away yet, because I needed to bid my time, being that I had some nasty injuries and didn't know for sure if I was in danger or with an ally.

I was being moved into an upright position, and when I felt my top being lifted, I gave a startled cry and batted the hands away. I opened my eyes to see a dark skinned boy staring at me, his eyebrows were bushy and his eyes were a very peculiar shade blue, which was very bright.

'How do you feel?' He asked, his voice was deep, yet there was something calming about it. He was wearing normal clothes, a green t-shirt and black jeans. Which confused me because what was he doing in the evil forest?

'Who are you and where am I?' I asked him, while looking at him warily. 'Not the right answer to my question.' he said with a grin.

'I feel as bad as I look.' I said hoping he would answer my own question 'I'm Kion and we're still in the cave of fears. I got to you just in time.' Kion said, opening a flask. 'I would like to know why you're here.' Kion said after a short while and I hadn't said anything.

I watched him pour some liquid into the cover of the flask, which made me curious 'What's that?' I asked, getting startled when smoke started to come up from the liquid. 'It's medicine. Here, it will help heal you,' Kion said and handed me the cover. I look down at the green liquid, which didn't look like it would stop bubbling.

'I'd advise you to drink it now. It doesn't work when it gets cold.' Kion said searching his backpack for something. I didn't want to drink it, but I knew if I wanted to get going I needed the pain to stop. Yet something about Kion felt trustworthy, I took a sip from the cup and spat out what I had in my mouth. It was the most disgusting thing I had ever tasted.

'It's disgusting, what's in it?'

'They are some special ingredients that aid in healing, mostly herbs. If you had taken it in one gulp, you wouldn't have tasted a thing.'

'I don't know.'

'You'll instantly feel better. Okay, how about this?' Kion took the cup from me gently. 'Here's the deal, I'll drink half of it first, and you drink the rest. Hopefully, we won't throw up.' he said with a laugh, which had me smiling.

'Deal,' I said and I watched him take a gulp from the cup, his face squeezed in disgust. I laughed at him, when he shuddered and handed the cup over to me. 'Your turn.' I closed my eyes, took a deep breath and swallowed the content of the cup in one gulp also. Kion was right. I barely tasted the concoction, but I felt a burning feeling cursing through me, after I had drank it, which had to be the healing effect of the medicine, doing its magic.

'Wasn't so bad, right? Kion asked rhetorically taking the cup from me. I nodded my head

'Here,' Kion said, as he brought out some bandages from his backpack. He motioned for me to remove my top, which I didn't have a problem with because I had a vest on and began working on my shoulder.

'Don't forget the leg and my head.' I reminded him and he nodded his head and said 'Don't worry, Doctor Kion, is here to save the day.' Which made us both laugh.

'So, I don't know your name…' Kion said and I offered my name up to him 'Annabelle.'

'That's a very nice name.'

'So Kion, where are you from?'

'South Africa. I moved to Nigeria three years ago.'

'And you live here?' I asked in alarm, because it was more than odd he lived in the forest.

'As if! This place is worse than any nightmare. I live in Abuja.'

'Then what are you doing here?' I asked, getting suspicious because all he had said wasn't adding up or explained why he was here.

He got up and put the flask in his bag, and then said cryptically 'Let's just say, the water led me.' he was hiding something and I didn't like that.

'We better get moving, before the spirits in this cave are able to sense our fears, because you and I do not want to face my fear.' He said as he put everything he had set out away and carried both of our backpacks.

'I can't leave without finding or knowing what has happened to my friends. What would I tell their parents if I left without getting answers. They are in this mess because they chose to help me.'

I said to Kion, who I'm sure wanted to get out of the cave and not lurk in it any more, as much as I also wanted to leave. I was loyal to my friends. Kion approached me as I attempted to get up and assisted me, once I was on my feet he didn't let me go.

'Look Ann, I know you care about your friends, but they're probably dead. You have been in this cave for hours.'

'But I still need to go—'

'Ann, it's your life you should be concerned about. It's hard to survive the cave of fears, and being caught means it's the end of whoever's life.'

'I'm still not leaving them.' I said, I wasn't going to go back on my words and take flight.

I looked at Kion, who was already staring at me. His eyes were actually beautiful and it was weird, how he had taken to calling me Ann, like we had been lifelong friends before today.

'If you're not going to change your mind, I'm going with you, I can't stomach the thought of you dying.'

Kion finally said with a long resigned sigh, which instantly made me happy and I sighed also, but with relief.

Chapter 8

'This place is so creepy.' I complained, as we passed through a dark, damp and rocky path, which made it hard to stay properly balanced, because I was constantly tripping.

'Oh, Princess Ann can't stand a little darkness?' Kion teased, he was walking smoothly, like it wasn't the uneven and rocky ground we were both navigating. He was so sure about his footing and it was like he knew how to move around the cave.

'Shut up.' I said and rolled my eyes at him, I made to move forward, when my foot sunk into mud, which was just great, my luck was now nonsense. I made to pull my foot out, but it didn't budge.

'Kion, I'm stuck!'

I cried out in annoyance, Kion looked down at my foot and frowned 'Don't worry we'll get you out.' Kion said right before he wrapped his arms around my waist and tried to carry me out, which was pointless because my foot didn't even budge.

We tried over and over again, but nothing was working, no matter how much strength Kion employed, the strangest thing though was the more Kion pulled, the more his muscles grew bigger.

He paused for a moment to catch his breath, he was exerting himself too much. 'Okay Princess Ann, you've got to hold onto me, I'm going to use all my strength on this next pull.' And he was right because with his last pull, he used so much strength, I felt my foot give and we both lost our footing and crashed into a wall, which gave and we landed on the ground.

Kion was groaning but he shook the pain off, got up and assisted me also. 'Well that definitely worked. Thank you.' I finally said, smiling at him in gratefully. Suddenly, the rocky path disappeared and we were now in a sort of room.

It was painted white from floor to ceiling, white pillars with gold sequence strewn all over it, symbols were written in gold on the ground and there were also gold shelves in every corner filled with jars which I was sure held strange items. One of the contents of a jar resembled an eyeball and I looked away in fright, because I was sure it was staring at me.

'Where is this?' I asked.

'We are in Otimesa's lair.' Kion said, also taking in the room. The place was both scary and beautiful, and I don't know how we were going to get out of it, because there was no visible exit.

'How are we going to get out? I don't see any opening.' I stated, which made Kion look at me. 'She doesn't need doors. She's probably a Zyton who can move through anything, and move anything through anything, if that makes sense. I didn't read that about her when I was learning her history.' Kion said indifferently, while surveying the symbols on the ground.

That was it, no more secrets. He had to tell me who he was and why he really was here. It wasn't a coincidence our paths crossed.

I was about to speak when I happened to look up and I let out a strangled scream. The ceiling that had looked plain before, was now made up of human beings that had been hung. They seemed to be wrapped up in some transparent looking silk, which resembled that of a spider's web.

'Kion, I think you're right about her being a Zyton.'

'Okay, I don't know about you, but I need to get out of here.'

Kion started frantically searching around hoping he could find a way out, but without looking I knew his search would be hopeless 'Where is Otimesa?' I calmly asked him, even though I felt anything but calm. It was strange how I had adjusted to the cold, especially with how cold this room was. I remembered what Kiola had said, about the cold being a sign of her presence. I vowed to myself that if I ever saw Kiola again, she would face my wrath.

'I don't know—'

'I'm right here.' a loud feminine voice interrupted Kion, who rushed to my side as we took in Otimesa's, she was a giantess, larger than life and made of gold. Her skin was gold, her hair was gold and cut short, but stylishly wavy on her head, her eyes and lips were startling white like her cloth, which was a white flowing gown, and they all blended perfectly with the white room. She had the form of a human, and looked like a beautifully sculpted statue.

'I thought I had gotten all who dared to enter my cave, up there but if I had known Geantoas had entered my cave, I would have doubled my effort.' Otimesa said smirking evilly at us.

That threw me for a loop and I chanced a glance at Kion, who was looking at Otimesa, he was also a Geantoa? Why hadn't he mentioned it? Everything was starting to make sense, for one he was a bit taller than I was, which was rare, and his formidable strength.

I was here on a mission and I wasn't going to back down now. 'Where are my friends?' I demanded from her, which brought her attention to focus on me. 'We meet at last, the infamous, Annabelle Nguma. I was expecting to see you.' she bitterly added 'Dead and decaying.'

I stepped forward ready to fight till my last breath but Kion moved in front of me, a sword in his hand, where had he produced that from? 'We only want the friends Otimesa.' Kion said with a self-assured confidence, confidence I knew I could only ever fake.

Otimesa looked at Kion like she was ready to squash him.

'I wouldn't protect her if I were you. She deserves to die. I am this close to being free from this hell. That's what I've been promised, in exchange for her life, and I won't let Geantoas ruin my plan!' Otimesa said her white eyes started to released white steam and I guess that's how she showed her anger.

Before I could blink Kion charged at Otimesa and I watched in awe because he started growing, rapidly becoming larger and taller and when he got to where she was he had become the same height as Otimesa, the momentum from his running had them falling heavily to the ground when he tackled her.

Kion was on top of her, he was about to bring his sword down on her chest, but Otimesa got the upper hand when something golden blasted from her hand and sent Kion flying off her and crashing into some shelves.

Otimesa was up on her feet immediately and started shooting golden bolts at Kion and my way, which we both were dodging. 'What are you doing wasting time? Transform now!' Kion bellowed at me, before he clashed his sword against Otimesa golden hand.

'Transform? What are you talking about?' I shouted back at Kion, who Otimesa had thrown across the room along with his sword. The crash made the whole room shake, even the humans up above where swinging and I hoped the thread holding them up didn't snap.

'You're a Geantoa! Transform!' Before I could ask him how I was meant to do that the room became very bright and became boiling hot 'Enough of this!' Otimesa screamed her voice resounding all through the room. 'I'm done with this child's play. You both are dead meat!' Her shout, was too loud and powerful the whole room rumbled. She stood still and started making a huge power ball, which she immediately launched at Kion, who didn't have enough time to dodge, Kion went crashing through the wall, leaving a smoky trail behind.

Watching Kion take such a brutal beating, unlocked something in me because I became so angry and I wanted to fight and protect him 'Leave him alone!' I screamed at Otimesa, who was playing with a small power ball and smirked at me before she said 'Make me.'

All I wanted to do was fight, so I started running towards her, when I started to transform. I felt my bones growing and my skin stretching and I knew I was growing, and I became even faster because Otimesa didn't know when I had jumped into the air and my fist slammed on her face.

The pain from hitting her face so hard wasn't much and it left as soon as it had come. I was back on my feet when Otimesa spat out gold liquid and glared at me with her white smoking eyes, wide in her eyes sockets, she hadn't expected me to have been the one to draw blood from her.

She stretched out her hands which began to morph and take on a different form, her hands became a sharp gold curved knives, which she started slashing at me, I didn't know where my the skill came from but my instinct took over and I backflipped out of the way.

Otimesa didn't pause and slashed at my arm, there was a cut but thankfully it wasn't deep, but I still winced in pain. I saw Kion's sword lying on the ground, near where he had crashed through, I hoped he was alright and would come through soon, if we wanted to get out of here, I had to defeat Otimesa.

I moved right before one of Otimesa's golden power ball hit me, I ran for the sword and grabbed it from the ground, now we had a somewhat equally baring. She charged at me, but I was prepared for her, when she tried to strike me with her arms, I held her off by kicking her in the stomach, which made her lose her balance.

Her collision with ground had a ground breaking impact and several cracks appeared where her body had settled. I rushed forward and pierced the sword into her chest. Her scream of outcry got cut off and the room became eerily silent.

I crashed to the floor, exhausted but triumphant that I had defeated her once and for all, but my triumphant feeling didn't last long because a crackling and purely evil laughter took the silence away and I was blasted into a wall, which had me screaming in pain at the impact.

To my horror, Otimesa still laughing drew the sword out of her and with her hands she melted the sword into nothing. 'At first, I was scared that it was the end for me, but they were right, you are clueless!'

Otimesa said, she was facing me now, her lips shaped in a deadly smile, her hands at her side started to light up, she was creating her power balls, I had to be ready to dodge them once she threw them.

What had I done wrong? Why wasn't she dead. Hadn't I pierced her heart? I took in Otimesa and she was completely fine, there was no blood or sign that I had pieced her skin with the sword. She threw another power ball at me and I easily dodged it. There had to be a way I could end her.

Water—

Water.

Water?

Water?

WATER!

The word kept repeating itself in my head and I did not know why, until I recalled a memory from my childhood. When I was younger, I always begged my parents to take me to the beach, Andrew and I would immediately run to the water and spend all our time playing in it, and sometimes our mum would join us. She had always said, water was important in her family, because it was her family's strength, and it would always protect us. I never understood how water would protect us and thought it was just a proverb, but she had been trying to tell us something.

It felt natural for me to drop onto my knees, and place my hands on the floor. I shut my eyes and took a deep breath *water is my family's strength, therefore, it is my strength.* I kept repeating the words until I couldn't hear anything, everywhere was quiet.

I thought hard about water, water in all its forms, water when it was calm and still, its harsh and dangerous waves when a storm was brewing, its spontaneous and beautiful waves when it was happy.

The water defines me.

It is my strength, my inner strength.

'My shrine! You are destroying it!' I opened my eyes because of Otimesa's shrieks and when I take in the room, it was flooded and was quickly filling up with more water. I was happy, because I knew what to do now. I stood up and raised my arm up and water jetted out of my hand. While I was marvelling over what I could do, Otimesa threw a power ball my way and out of reflex I held up my hands, waiting for the impact but nothing happened, when I looked up I saw why. I had created a water wall and it was holding the shimmering ball of power back from colliding with me.

'Nooo!' Otimesa screamed, when I smiled and with all my might I pushed at the ball with my water shield and it went flying back to meet its creator, who wasn't fast enough and crashed into her shelves.

I needed to slay her now once and for all, since I had water now to use as a powerful weapon. I needed another sword or knife anything I could use to pierce her skin and take the life out of her. I was thinking hard, when water rose from the ground and started to form a shape, when it was half way through, I realised what was being made, the water was making a sword for me. The sword was transparent like water and it's hilt had some symbols on it which I couldn't analyse. The moment I held it in my hand, I felt a powerful surge from it, as it pulsed with so much energy.

I waddled as fast as I could over to Otimesa unconscious form and immediately thrust the sword down on her, it was her face I had hit, I had used so much force, I had spilt her head in two.

The temperature in the room changed instantly, it was no longer freezing cold and it now felt cool, and soothing to the skin. I watched as the parts of Otimesa's body that were white turn gold including her dress, she remained still and unmoving, staring blankly at nothing. The sword also disintegrated into mere water and ran down her body. I was completely exhausted and I had no energy left, I stumbled and started falling when something…more like someone caught me and I looked up to see it was Kion.

'Sorry I wasn't here to help, but I'm glad you know what you are and are capable of.'

Kion softly says, he looked like he was beating himself over the fact that he hadn't been very useful at the end.

'Hey. It is not your fault. She was pretty powerful and trust me, it wasn't easy at all.'

'But you handled her well—'

'It was luck. I didn't even know I could do that, and I don't even know who I am anymore.' I said resigned and Kion and I settled into an uncomfortable silence.

'It's hard at first, but you'll learn to live with it.' Kion said.

We both looked down at Otimesa's body and I asked 'Do you think she's gone forever?'

'No, she will have to remain in the underworld for some centuries, but she will eventually return in a new form, she can never escape from her curse.' I shuddered and looked up at the ceiling, we had to get all these people down.

'Let's get your friends and leave, we shouldn't spend any more time in this cursed place.' Kion said, having the same thoughts as I was. Kion and I were still in our gigantic forms, so we could easily pluck down the people, who were like tiny toys in our hands. They were still unconscious, I held my friends and some other people in my hands, being very careful so I didn't crush them.

The last person Kion freed was a blue creature that resembled Kiola, but I knew it wasn't her, which made me surer that Kiola had betrayed me in some way.

Immediately we were done, the room started to shake violently and I asked Kion alarmed 'What is happening?' Kion started running for the exit he had created when he crashed into the wall earlier. 'The cave is coming down! Run!' he screamed at me, leading the way as we dodged falling rocks, I think being a Geantoa made us really fast, because we were out of the cave faster than I thought was possible and while we were panting, a huge rock fell inside and blocked the entrance to the cave.

'Whoa, that was super close.' Kion lamely supplied and I nodded my head in agreement.

I was bent over, clutching my knees, and panting, when something shiny caught my attention and I had a feeling it was a gem, when I got closer I was right, it was a yellowish coloured jewel, which I quickly picked up, like the first one while I held it in my palms it dissolved and disappeared but I wasn't worried or alarmed like I had been when the first gem disappeared.

I had two more gems to go and I would seal and free myself from Ezyron and his minions forever. I stood up to see Kion was back to his normal size and build, he was oblivious to what I had just discovered and I felt a pang of guilt, because I was keeping my mission and why I was here a secret from him, but he also wasn't telling me everything, so I couldn't completely trust him, even though I felt he was a good person.

'Hey Kion. How do I return back to a moderate size?'

I asked right before I sat down gently on the ground. I stretched out my palms towards Kion, who gladly climbed on to it. 'All you have to do is to relax, and be at peace.' he said, and he jumped off from my palm, showing off. I took in a deep breath and slowly released it, I did that a couple of times and when I opened my eyes I was human sized again.

'That was easier than I thought.' I said very pleased with myself, which had Kion shaking his head and smiling at me. 'Yes it's easy, but it's also easy to grow if you don't learn to control your temper. Geantoas become giants, when they sense they are in danger, or when they are livid, so it's good practicing how to stay calm.'

I wondered again how Kion had so much knowledge about the

spiritual world, he's very comfortable with who he was. I watched him move to one person or creature after the other and force fed them the liquid from his flask, but I couldn't help questioning him.

'What you're saying is if I get even the tiniest bit angry or afraid, I would grow?'

'See Ann, it's normal you're still discovering yourself and learning to deal with this new reality of yours, so don't hold it against yourself, if you can't control it, it takes years to control ourselves, even older Geantoas who have years of practice, sometimes find it hard to have control.'

He clearly had control over his growth spurt and the only time I had seen him angry was when Otimesa was attacking us.

'When will my friends wake up?' I finally said, because we needed to get going, if I wanted to locate the other gems and protect the world from Ezyron.

'Any moment now Ann, I believe this is where we part ways. I have to lead and protect this people, make sure they return back to where they came from or find a safe place for them, because time is no more and Ezyron would rise soon. I don't know who or what will stop it.'

The sky was dark and gloomy, I took a chance and checked my phone and to my horror, the clock display was going crazy and just spiralling, showing different numbers, but not actually telling the time.

Ezyron was getting more and more powerful with each second I stood here wasting time.

'You know about Ezyron?' I asked him, hoping he would tell me more about himself or the evil forest.

Kion looked at me like he couldn't believe I asked such a question before he spoke 'You can't be in the evil forest and not know about

Ezyron, more than half of the occupants are afraid of him and the rest are his loyalists.'

'Yes, I have encountered many strange creatures, who couldn't help but scream in glee, Ezyron was coming and the world would suffer.' I decided to give him a little bit of my truth, without giving my purpose away.

'It's because the prophecy states no one apart from the evil spirits in the forest know who or what will bring down Ezyron. But now he is presumed to be dead since the countdown to the end has started.'

I wasn't dead and I was a she, not he. Kion hands his flask over to me, saying I should keep it in case of emergencies, since I didn't know how to brew the potion or knew what plants I would need in the first place. The people he had given the drinks were showing signs of life again, because their skin wasn't as pale as it was when we had first escaped.

He stood and whistled loudly.

'What are you doing?' I asked in alarm 'You'll see.' Was all Kion said and smiled at me.

A huge gust of wind rushed out from nowhere, stirring up the sand and bending trees backwards, it was so powerful it unbalanced me and I fell on my butt.

Flying in the sky was a huge creature, which was blue and black in colour, with a long tail, the tail itself was dangerous looking, it was covered with spikes, even though some of their pointy tips had been chirped off. The scariest thing about the creature though, was when it landed and I got to view it's head, it had the head of a snake, a cobra to be exact and to make it worse its eyes had different colours, one was white and the other blue, like Kion's eyes.

Couldn't we catch a break in this forest? The creature raised its head and looked me dead in my eyes, as it started to fold its leathery wings and I became frozen to the spot, but Kion was comfortable and he moved towards the creator, and started stroking it's head, and it started to hiss. That creature was hissing in pleasure and I was baffled.

'Ann come and meet Ife.' Kion urged me to come over, it took me some seconds, but I finally found the courage to move closer and join Kion 'Don't be scared, she won't harm you.' Obviously he would say that, they clearly had a bond, where as I was a stranger to the creature.

'It's hard to believe, but she is an herbivore, she only eats plants, even though yes she can breathe fire, and can be very deadly, when she is engaged in a combat. But she isn't the slightest bit carnivorous or an omnivore.' As if Ife could understand what he was saying, she licked his face, which was both intriguing and shocking to see.

Reluctantly I covered the few steps it would take me to be within touching distance of the monster and reached out my hand. Its skin was rough to the touch and I yanked my hand away in fear.

'Your hand seems fine to me.' Kion said before he laughed and continued to stroke the monster called Ife.

'We really need to get going.' I said hoping he would leave already, I wasn't comfortable with that creature.

'How are you exploring the forest?' Kion asked.

'By foot, of course.'

'You don't have a Serpent? You've been traipsing all over this forest by foot?' Kion asked with so much shock in his voice.

'Well, I just—'

'Ann, weren't you told? The ground is more dangerous than the air. How could they send you into the forest without preparing you or teaching you anything? That was very unwise and I'm angry on your behalf.' he ranted to me.

You're as clueless as ever. A voice that resembled Otimesa's rang out loud inside my head.

'It seems like fate, I ran into you. I'll share Ife with you.' Kion went on speaking, which pulled me up short when he said the last bit. I didn't want to be near his creature and now he wanted to share it with me, when he also needed it to leave.

'You don't have to do that, you also need Ife.'

'I said share her with you.'

'How would you do that?'

'Ife, clone!' Kion commanded Ife, who was staring at me.

Ife closed its creepy eyes for a second and when it opened again, both pupils were black. For some odd reason, Ife started melting, until it was a pool of thick black liquid oil. The liquid separated into two and began to take the forms of the Serpent.

It was creepy yet amazing to witness the Serpent cloning itself.

'You know how reptiles shed their skins? Well Serpents clone themselves, but the clones eventually dry out and disappear. The clones are equally as powerful as the real Serpent, but how long they are around for solely depends on how strong the original Serpent is. Ife is very strong, and her clones always last for thereabout three days.'

Kion informed me, I couldn't even spare him a glance because the creatures, had captured my attention and I was still in awe.

'Ife, carriage!' Kion commanded again and a black carriage, which seemed to be attached to Ife's skin formed on its back.

Kion stood still and started growing, once he was as big as he wanted to be, he lifted the people, he was taking away and placed them in the carriage one after the other, before he shrunk and got in the carriage.

'Farewell Princess Ann! I really hope we meet again!' He shouted down at me, and I bid him farewell, I really hoped our paths crossed again.

'Take care!' His final words of farewell, echoed back at me, as Ife flew away with him and his passengers.

I turned to face my Serpent and named it Nife, which it apparently liked, because it let out a satisfied purr, when I called it that.

Chapter 9

'This is bad, this is so bad!' Mara shouted, as we flew higher up in the sky and were now above the clouds.

'No kidding. We're all going to die before this thing kills us because of you.'

Mike said dryly, his faced squeezed together in pain. Mara was clutching his arm and her fingernails were now embedded in his skin.

When my friends came to and discovered we were soaring through the sky, they all had different reactions. Nodebe and Mara were scared, and it was very hard trying to calm them down. Mike and Zina were indifferent to it, and looked around and tried studying Nife, in awe, while Zoe started sulking, being the ever annoying and entitled brat she was.

Especially after I explained our situation, she did all but called me stupid, because we had no weapon and Nife, would eventually fade away. It made me angry because, of how ungrateful she was being, I had risked everything to save everyone. They didn't even know I had

had help, it didn't occur to them to think about what I must have gone through to save them and get them out of the cave before we were trapped inside forever.

'Are we there yet? Tell me we're there.' Nodebe said, he was shivering like he was in a bath filled with ice, but it was his fear that had gotten the best of him.

'Zoe, stop kicking me!' Mara wailed

'You, stop leaning on me!' Zoe snapped back at Mara.

'Mara! I really like my blood in my body!' Mike took the opportunity to add his own raised voice and complain.

'Take me down! Take me down!' Nodebe started shouting, while tears freely flowed from his eyes, adding to the chaos of voices.

They were all so ungrateful, and they were making me agitated. I had liked it when it was just Kion and I, he was easy to talk to, he understood me and always listened to what I had to say, the respect we had for one another was clear. I missed his company more than ever, and if I was being honest, I would rather him being with me, than my so called friends.

I was still stewing about my friends in silence when I felt a hand on my shoulder. Thinking it was someone who was about to pick a fight I whirled around very fast to face the culprit and asked coldly.

'What?'

But it was Zina, who looked at me sheepishly and with remorse in his eyes.

'What?' I repeated again, more gently.

'Thank you, for saving us.' He said.

He was the only grateful one, the only one would had sense and was always in tune with how I was feeling, it was sad he and Zoe were together. I nodded my head in acknowledgement and his lips started to form a grin which broke out into a smile.

'We need to get some weapons.' Zina said, staring down at the clouds.

'Maybe we can find a group of people who can help us.' I said and asked Nife.

'Nife, we need weapons, do you know where we can find?'

It blew smoke from its nose. 'I guess, that's a yes.' I said to Zina who had now moved to sit beside me.

'Hey!' someone shouted, Zina and I turned around to see Mara practically on Mike with her arms wrapped tightly around his waist. 'Are we there yet? I don't think I can handle her anymore.' Mike said breathlessly.

Nife let out a roar and breathed fire into the air, which had my alerts sharpening but looking around I didn't spy anything that could be classified dangerous, but Nife had moved below the clouds and I could see why it had let out the warning, below on the ground I could make out a few huts of different sizes.

The ride back to earth was fast and we all had to hold on to the carriage, while Nife headed for the ground in full speed, but when we were about to hit the floor, it pulled up and gently landed.

Mike had to carry Mara off with him, and she immediately sunk to the floor and said 'Adding heights to my list of fears.'

'Well, add Mara to my list of fears!' Mike half-jokingly said.

The moment the last person got off Nife, the carriage disappeared. I walked to where it's head was and rubbed it affectionately, which made it hiss.

'Try and stay hidden until I signal for you.' I whispered to Nife, and immediately she took off. I turned back to my friends and called out 'Hey Mara!' She looked at me with confusion and I smiled before I said 'How about you lead us through this part of the forest?'

We had walked for a bit, when Zoe's voice rang out, she had just tripped over a fallen branch and was flustered. 'How much farther is the place? I'm tired of this place!' Zina who had returned back to her side, helped her back on her feet.

'I'd advise you to be quiet.' Mara said and carefully climbed over a branch while studying the map.

'And I'd advise you to be a better leader.' Zoe hotly threw back at Mara.

'We don't need an argument now.' I said, wearily. I was starting to feel the effect of all my activeness and I was starting to lag a bit behind.

Mike was the first to notice and called out to me 'You okay, Annabelle?' He had stopped and was waiting for me to catch up. Which made the others aware, because they all stopped and turned back to look at me.

'I'm fine, just a bit tired,' I called back, but I was much more tired than I had initially thought because I tripped and went down, I didn't even have the energy to catch myself.

Mike and Zina rushed to my side and with their support I was able to get back up, but they didn't let me go and insisted on remaining at my side to support me.

'Hey, guys come and see what I found.' Mara shouted a bit far ahead.

'Oh goodie, more walking, tripping and falling, yay!' Zoe said sarcastically and kicked at a fallen branch. We were all moving towards where Mara was when I noticed something bright in Nodebe hands, and upon further inspection it looked like a book.

'Nodebe, what do you have there?' Zina asked, after following my line of sight. Nodebe was startled by the question but answered 'Nothing.'

Zina asked Nodebe again with a much firmer voice and Nodebe slowly turned around. Sure enough, the book in his hand was PRISONOMIA. How he had gotten his hands on it again was unclear to me because, it should have been left abandoned in the Cave of Fears.

'How did you get it?' I suspiciously asked.

Nodebe looked at the book first and was lost in thought before looking back at us. 'I found it in a tree. I took it out and was equally as surprised as you are, when it was the book. It's following me.' he said, and the way he held the book to his chest made me uncomfortable, because he was cradling it like a baby.

'Let's catch up with the others.' Mike said.

Which reminded us we had somewhere to get to and time wasn't on our side. We started moving once again but my mind remained on Nodebe and the book, something wasn't right, with how attached he was to the book. Why the book selected him.

He had also said, he had seen the book in a tree, like I had seen it the first time, but I knew if I asked, Nodebe would just shrug it away and not give me the answer I sought.

Zoe and Mara were distressed, which made me apprehensive, something wasn't right. The stench that was coming from this area was very sickening, it was horrible and I covered my nose with a hand, hoping to filter the smell.

'What's wrong?' Mike asked them.

Mara didn't look at us, or in the direction she pointed to. We moved towards the bush by our left and unconsciously made the decision to look together.

There were bones everywhere and badly decomposing bodies. Many of the skeletal remains, showed that the people who been killed, had been gruesomely killed. Fractured skulls, ribs, some of the bodies still had the weapons that had been used to kill them, embedded in them. It looked like a massive burial site, or more like dumping site for the deceased.

We remained in shock, as we took in the horrible site before us. I couldn't even speak if I wanted to, because I felt the instant my mouth opened I would throw up, because the sight had somehow heightened the stench.

'Man down.' Zoe said.

We heard a thud and turned around, Mara had fainted. Mike rushed to Mara's side and lifted her from the ground, and hitched her over his shoulder.

I thanked Mike for his quick thinking, and he nodded his head in acknowledgement, Mara had grown on him it seemed.

'Are you still sure about going to the village?' Nodebe asked.

'Yes, we should still go. We need weapons and food. Who knows? It could be those who committed crimes in the village.' I responded and freed myself from Zina and picked up the discarded map from the floor.

'That's a lot of people.' Zina blurted out, trying to make me change my mind. But I wasn't going to.

'Then, I guess we better be on our best behaviours.' I said and began walking, leading the way, I had regained some of my strength back and was able to lead without dragging everyone else.

After a while, I looked back, and saw Zoe stumble over another fallen branch, and instead of getting back up she sat on the ground, halting all our movements.

'You okay, Zoe?' Zina asked, I moved closer and noticed she looked sick, she had gotten quiet while we walked, which wasn't like her, since she had been complaining from the moment we landed.

'No. I have a terrible headache.' she said clutching at her head.

Zina looked at me with pleading eyes, but we really didn't have any more time to spare, and needed to keep moving.

'We need to keep moving. Carry her if she can't walk.'

Zina was about to help Zoe back on her feet when she screamed. The scream was so loud and jarring, we all flinched and immediately protected our ears.

The scream was peculiar because it consisted of different tones. Zoe got up on her feet and began to hit Zina furiously. She swiped a long stick and brandished it like a weapon, pointed at Zina.

'Don't ever touch me!' she said maliciously, before turning to face me. Her pupils were grey now and her eyes looked so lifeless. She looked up at the sky and let out another horrible scream.

Different versions of her terrible scream, echoed back at her and she smiled, before shouting 'My People!' we were all now cowering and covering our ears. She growled and started running in my direction. I knew I had to stop her, but I also knew she wasn't herself, so I moved aside and she ran past me and disappeared.

• • •

'Ezyron has to be behind all of this.' Mike stated, we were panting as we were walking on uneven ground. We all knew Ezyron was behind all of it, he didn't want us to succeed, so of course he was going to sabotage all our plans and waste away our efforts.

'Where exactly would she have run to?' Mara asked, she was moving slowly and being careful about where she stepped on. She had come around when Zoe had been screaming.

'She ran in this direction, and the path we are on is cleared, so it's the safest bet.' I said observing the environment.

'But doesn't this road lead to the village?' Mara said staring at me.

Mike perked up when Mara asked her question and I nodded yes. I hoped Zoe would be at the village and also not harm anyone, and make it hard for us to rescue her.

'My head, legs, tummy and everywhere hurts! Are we there yet?' Nodebe shouted out of the blue, which had some birds up in some trees, fly away due to the disturbance, it was so childish and uncalled for, because his shout could have alerted the people of the village we were coming, and I wasn't sure if we would be met with hostility or kindness.

'Will you shut up? You asked for an adventure and you got it, nothing is fair in this—' Mara interrupted my ranting, when she slapped her hand over my mouth and I realized I had grown. They were all staring up at me with stunned expressions. I calmed myself down and also shrunk back to my average height.

'Sorry, let's just get Zoe, the weapons, and the gems, lock up Ezyron and get out of here. This place is beginning to mess with us.' I said and continued moving.

We walked a short distance, tripping and falling, quarrelling and silently cursing at one another, when we heard the rhythmic beating of drums.

'What's the celebration for?' Zina asked.

'Whatever the celebration is, it means we came on a good day.' Mike replied.

We could see some sort of clearing in front, where the villagers may have gathered. The whole area was brightly lit, colourful lanterns had been hung on the old muddy hut with thatched roofs. The hut I was close to looked dazzling with different symbols and animals carved on its body. It looked like the building was trying to tell a story.

The women wore only wrappas, which they had tied around their chests while the young girls tied one wrappa round their chest which didn't reach their midriffs and the other tied to their small waists and fell to their knees. The men had wrappas tied around their waist and wore beads of different shapes while the young boys wore almost the same thing except there was a strap of cloth over their body joined to the waist cloth.

They looked primed and ready for something, the excitement in the air could easily be seen.

'What's the commotion about?' Mike asked me, but I was equally as clueless as he was.

'I don't know. But it's better if we stay behind and out of view, so we can observe them, without alerting them of our presence yet.' I said and moved closer, but was using the huts to protect me from being seen.

The music stopped and a dark stout middle-aged man, dressed in a wrappa around his waist and a red scarf on his head and white and black marks painted on half of his face, stood to address the crowd, when a group started to sing a slow mournful song in their language. Once it ended, the man cleared his throat.

'People of Ulogboro, I, Chief Izinwa Ogbosi Agbalakumu, welcome you on this fine day as we celebrate with our queen. Today is the day, our lioness mated with her lion. The day the bee found its flower. The day the bird found the tree. For years, we suffered by the hands of the witch, Nameless!' Shouts and murmurs of displeasure erupted from the crowd at his statement, the people were lamenting and it was clear whoever the Nameless witch was, she had dealt with them badly.

Chief Izinwa raised his hand and the crowd became silent and continued speaking 'Yes, I know you are all worried and anxious, but her reign is over. Our queen is finally free from bondage—' the crowd erupted in cheers, he waited for them to calm down again before he went on. 'Now, I present to you our priceless jewel. Our lioness, the eyes, ears, and mouth of our land, the most powerful woman in the land, Queen Olosinwe!'

The drums started playing a loud and rhythmic beat, that had the crowd dancing in jubilation. A group of girls danced their way through the crowd which parted, for them, because following behind the dancers were four big men carrying a throne from all four corners.

There were golden curtains preventing us from seeing the queen. The men set the throne down, where Chief Izinwa had been addressing the crowd. The people of Ulogboro knelt down and bowed their heads when their queen stood up from her throne.

The queen was truly a sight to behold. Placed on her head was a beaded crown, her dark skin gleamed beautiful in the bright sun light. Her eyes were big and her face was warm and welcoming, she was adorned all over with beaded jewelleries and wrapped around her chest was a velvet wrappa, that went down to the ankles of her feet.

'My queen.' Chief Izinwa said and bowed.

The queen looked out at her people and smiled, her smile was so bright and blinding, because of how it further transformed her into a glowing beauty.

'Rise my people, you have all served me well.' She said and raised her hands motioning for them all to rise. 'I am happy to be here with you all on this joyous day to celebrate the end of NAME—' Queen Olosinwe was interrupted by a wild crackle of laughter, which immediately had the tension in the air change from joyous to fearful and silence befell the people.

Queen Olosinwe looked at Izinwa before surveying the crowd, her smile was wiped from her face and was replaced with a fierce look. The sky started rapidly changing, from bright and sunny to dark and cloudy.

'We better leave. I have a bad feeling about this.' Mike whispered to me, looking up at the sky.

'We can't. We need to get weapons and find Zoe.' I said, not looking away from the queen.

Suddenly, one of the men, who had brought the queen on her throne approached her, he had a white wrappa tied around his waist, and also adorned jewels made from beads on his wrists and neck. He looked young and virile but a bit older than the queen, and even from where I was I could tell he was very handsome.

'My Queen isn't safe. She must leave.' he said, worry lines forming on his face.

'No my love. I have to stay, it's my duty to our people and the gods have willed it.' she said and closed her eyes.

'My queen, you can't—'

'Oloshorun, you can't tell me what I can or can't do. I've made up my mind. Something is disturbing my land, I will stay and protect it the best way I can. The gods promised me a saviour.' Queen Olosinwe said, and kissed Oloshorun on the lips.

'Wasn't that the sweetest.' a shrill feminine voice dripping with derision said, which set off cries of displeasure from the crowd, the couple had broken apart and Queen Olosinwe had come to stand in front of Oloshorun, in a protective stance.

Someone in a long black cloak broke away from the crowd and approached the Queen, the person stopped a feet away from the Queen.

'You couldn't have forgotten about me so soon?' The cloaked

figure said and Queen Olosinwe eyes widened and she asked in a whisper 'Nameless?'

'I am undefeatable. How foolish to think you a mere mortal can get rid of Nameless. I am no one and everyone. I can be nowhere and everywhere. You merely weakened me, but now I have found the perfect host. This body I have taken will sustain me and now I can destroy you and your people once and for all.'

Lightning flashed and thunder struck, the cloak flew away and revealed who was behind the eerie voice, when I saw who it was the others and I let out a gasp. It was Zoe.

Zoe had raided somebody's home because she was dressed like the people of Ulogboro a black wrappa was tied around her chest, a grey and red wrappa was tied around her small waist, which flowed down below her knees and she had beads on her neck and her waist. She had drawn on her face as well little black dot from her forehead down to her chin in straight line. Even though she was pure evil right now, she still looked beautiful, and it made me sick. I glanced over at Zina, who was staring at his girlfriend with shock and awe plastered all over his face.

'Nameless. Let the child be. She has nothing to do with this.' Queen Olosinwe said calmly, but her voice was as sharp as the steel of a sword.

'Her negativity is the best, it feeds and powers me. I will never give her up.' Nameless said, it was strange to see Nameless take command of Zoe's body, watching Zoe's mouth move, but another being's voice come out, was very shocking.

Queen Olosinwe nodded at two of her guards who charged at Nameless, but she was expecting them, with a flick of her finger in their direction, they were engulfed in flames. The crowd screamed and had started running for cover when, Nameless faced the crowd and waved her hands, movement stopped and the people of Ulogboro became frozen to the spot.

'Stay people of Ulogboro! Where do you think you're running to?'

I wasn't frozen, neither were my friends, who were checking to see if they had been affected.

Queen Olosinwe eyes turned as dark as coal, she walked gracefully like she was threatened towards where the burnt guards were and picked up the sword of one of the fallen warriors.

She stood straight and stared hard at Nameless 'For the last time leave!' Queen Olosinwe shouted, with so much volume, I winced, but Nameless just gestured with her hand for her to bring it on.

Queen Olosinwe charged at Nameless, who didn't flinch or looked like she was scared. When the Queen was close enough, Nameless grabbed and slammed her onto the ground before throwing her against a nearby hut.

'Sinwe!' Oloshorun shouted in fear, but charged at Nameless in anger. Nameless let out a laugh and watched him approach, she didn't say anything but flick her finger and Oloshorun became engulfed in her deadly flames.

The frozen people of Ulogboro still had use of their mouth, and the outcry from them, watching their Queen's beloved burn to his death, was painful and heart wrenching to hear.

Nameless, danced to their cries for a short bit, before she waved her hands at the people and took away their voices, making everywhere quiet, except from the sound of rustling leaves, and animals.

The Queen, regained consciousness and struggled a bit, but got back on her feet, she was ready to face Nameless again, when she noticed Oloshorun, who was now a burnt carcass on the ground, she went down on her knees and let out a blood curling scream of sorrow. With all her might Queen Olosinwe threw her sword at Nameless, who stopped the weapon long before it reached her and I watched it splinter into a thousand pieces.

It was pointless, why were they still attacking Nameless, when she could destroy them all without moving from where she was. Surprisingly, Queen Olosinwe threw her hand up and a wall sprouted out the earth, blocking the metal ball from hitting her. I was so shocked to see she had such powers but the people were not shocked. Obviously, this infuriated Nameless.

A wall made from mud grew from the ground, it was so fast, Nameless couldn't protect herself and she went falling to the ground. It was the Queen's doing and it surprised me, and my friends. I was worried about Zoe, even though Nameless had taken over her body, she was still worth saving.

'Stupid child! Your power won't save you!' Nameless shouted, but was still unsettled by the fall, Queen Olosinwe wasn't wasting time, and a glass enclosing grew from the ground and enclosed Nameless, I watched in awe has the enclosing started to shrink and also did Nameless, who seemed to be trapped and couldn't break free.

'I will crush you to dust.' Queen Olosinwe said, but speaking had broken her concentration, because Nameless had managed to break the glass, cracked lines started forming and with a loud sound, the glass shattered and Nameless stood straight, an evil smirk on her face.

'Nice, but I can do better.' Nameless said.

Nameless twirled her finger in a circular motion and a ring of fire flared up entrapping the Queen in its centre, returning the favour, the space within the fire started to reduce, and we knew the Queen, would perish by fire.

'Say goodbye to your beloved Queen!' Nameless roared and

was about to burn the Queen, when someone I would never have expected intervened.

'Stop please!' Mara shouted, running in front of Nameless, who was startled by Mara, she had frozen the whole village and taken away their voices, yet there stood Mara, who had on clothes that were different, bravely approaching her.

I was proud of Mara, who looked as tough as ever, she was a mess, yet she wasn't breaking down. Her clothes were torn in some places, and her skin was grimy with dirt.

'Zoe, please don't do this. This isn't you. You're not that mean.' Mara said with pleading eyes. This didn't move Nameless, who started smirking.

'I do not bear the name Zoe—' I knew Mara was screwed, so I started sneaking towards Nameless, while she concentrated on Mara 'You're disrupting and I don't like that.'

I snuck up on her, when she was about to wave a finger at Mara and tackled her to the ground, I was growing angrier by the second and so was my body. The moment I had tackled her, the fire enclosing the Queen went out, and the people of Ulogboro unfroze, her power was in her hands, and if I could keep her from using them, everyone would be safe.

Nameless did not give up, she pushed at the ground with her hands, which created a powerful blast that threw me away from her, quickly she waved her hands around and everything became dark.

• • •

I woke up with a start, because of a loud startling sound. Someone was banging something on metal. I tried to sit up, and when my eyes came into focus I saw Mike was the culprit hitting a stone against metal bars. I looked around and spotted Mara crying in one corner, and Nodebe lying down at another corner, he was asleep.

Zina and Zoe, were not with us, which was a scary thought and I had to asked 'Where is Zina?'

'Annie! Thank God, you're awake. We need to get out now. Zoe or Nameless is going to kill us if we don't escape.' Mara nervously informed me, she had come to me and was now crying on my shoulder. 'I don't think I can do this anymore Annabelle.'

I was tired, a dirty mess and if I was being honest mentally unstable. I hated it, but I knew I had no choice but to be brave, because I was never normal to begin with.

'Mara, please stop crying, I promise you I will end this nightmare.' I said though I doubt that I sounded convincing, but gradually Mara's crying slowed to a stop and she finally wiped her face with her shirt.

Mike dropped the stone, which crashed to the floor and drew my attention to him, He looked terrible, he had cuts all over his arms, his lips were swollen and it looked like he had been burned on his cheek.

'I shouldn't have volunteered. I could be at home doing something fun, instead of waiting for someone to kill me. Why did I agree to this!' He lamented mostly to himself, before slumping beside the metal bars.

I couldn't find it in me to try and make Mike feel better, I hadn't forced anyone to come with me, they had all insisted, but I was also tired.

I was here because of my parents, it was their decision that became our family's ultimate downfall and now I had no choice but to right everything, even though I had no hand in causing it.

I had to be brave, we hadn't come this far, to give up now. We were better than this and we could outsmart Nameless, I just had to think.

'There has to be a way out.' I said at last, with renewed hope.

'I don't think so. We are doomed.' Mike said.

'Give the Geantoa a chance.' A familiar feminine voice said. I hadn't seen another person in the cell, so I whirled around and was surprised when I took in the form of Queen Olosinwe. I hadn't dared to think of what had happened the people of Ulogboro, but if their Queen was still alive, perhaps there still was hope for them.

'You are worthy and ready, Geantoa.' the Queen said to me, she had cuts on her face, but despite the marks, she was still a beauty to look at her, but most importantly the regal air about her remained.

'How do you know I'm a Geantoa?' I asked.

Queen Olosinwe was about to speak, but she paused, before she finally said. 'Your eyes are not like the rest.'

'Yes, my eyes turned white when, I got into this forest.'

She shook her head and smiled, Mike and Mara, came closer and took a look at my face before they let out a surprised gasp.

'What is it?' I asked, what had my eyes done again?

'Your eyes, they're …um … well, we didn't even notice. But,' Mara stammered and she was getting me agitated.

'They're now blue. Except I can't tell the type of blue. It's really bright though.' Mike said and I was grateful because Mara would have kept me in suspense for God knew how long.

'It's okay Annabelle. I am also a Geantoa, but not of your kind. It is difficult to accept at first, but it grows on you and you function better when you accept it.' Queen Olosinwe cuts in which didn't surprise me, because I had guessed so, but what threw me was the fact there were various kinds of Geantoa?

My eyes were blue? Like Kion's eyes? Were we the same kind of Geantoa? He had said the water had led him and I had discovered that water was also my strength.

Queen Olosinwe was watching me, and it was eerie, because I felt like she could tell I was slowly piecing it all together. She reached out a hand to press down on my shoulder comfortingly.

I looked at her eyes now and saw my bright blue eyes in hers, her pupils colour were different shades of bright green. I wished I could ask more about being a Geantoa, but now wasn't the time.

'How do we get out of here?' I asked her, this was her land, she had to know something.

'You will get us out of here, with your innate connection with water. My powers are useless here, because my powers have been sealed, so I can't escape from this cell.'

'You mean her growing into a giant?' Nodebe corrected the Queen, it was true they didn't know I had discovered I had another hidden talent. Mike and Mara agreed with Nodebe, so I knew I was about to shock them.

'I need water.' I said.

Queen Olosinwe smiled, 'water flows underground, you can harness the water from there. But do you know how you're going to do it?'

'We'll know, once I give it a try.' I asked for room and everyone moved backwards. I pressed my hand to the ground and calmed myself down by evening my breathing. I called for the water below and willed it to listen and obey me.

I felt the water rushing up from below, I raised my hand up and water left the ground and was in sync with my hand movement, with deep concentration, I focused on the bars and the water moved in between two bars and widening until a hole big enough for us to climb out of our cell appeared.

'Whoa! Ann, you're some kind of superhero!' Mike said, the awe in his voice surprised me and made me smile. Mara and Nodebe looked equally surprised, the relief we all felt, about being able to get out, had all of us including Queen Olosinwe smiling.

'Let's leave now. The ceremony has begun and the guards will soon come and get us.' the Queen said hastily, and we all filed out of the cell.

'What about weapons? We can't go there unarmed.' Nodebe said, pulling on my arm.

'I will lead you to the weapons room. All I know is it's you Geantoa, who would defeat Nameless once and for all. It's the only information the gods shared with me. When you get your weapons, I will leave you and your friends, I will hold off the guards, from following you.'

While we were hurriedly rushing through the prison two guards apprehended us.

'The prisoners! After them!' One of the guards said, and they began running towards us.

'Go!' Queen Olosinwe shouted at us, since she was no longer in the cell, her powers had been restored, she created an earth wall to lock the guards from coming after us, she then took the lead and led us out of the prison and into the forest.

'I didn't know we were locked in the forest.' Mara said panting for air.

'Our prisons are underground and away from our main village.' Queen Olosinwe said and we all kept quiet after that, she led us to a gated part in the forest and in front of it were two guards, who were keeping intruders out, they didn't have time to raise the alarm, because Queen Olosinwe immediately smacked the guards in the head with two earth balls, which made them go unconscious.

Beyond the wall, was a big hut, and inside it was incredible. Everywhere in it were different weapons, the walls were decorated with different symbols and animals. It was lit by torches, which made the weapons glow even brighter.

'This is amazing.' I said and Queen Olosinwe stands taller and is clearly proud of her weaponry.

'Thank you. We do have the best blacksmiths here. Choose you weapons and let's leave.' Queen Olosinwe said hastily, watching the door. I grabbed a sword while Mara grabbed a bow and a sling filled with arrows. I watched Mike who grabbed a sword with a snake on the hilt.

Nodebe didn't look around for a weapon, he held up the PRISONOMIA book, I hated the book, something about it gave me goose bumps.

'We better get weapons for Zina and Zoe. We might not be able to come back.' Mara said, grabbing another bow and sling of arrows. Mike grabbed another sword, and I looked around in case there was anything else we needed.

'Daggers just in case.' I said.

I grabbed a dagger, when I saw a shield with symbols that called to me craved on it. The symbols were representing water, earth, fire and air. It called to me for some reason I could not explain so I grabbed it as well and hung it on my back, thanks to the strap attached to it.

'We're ready!' I said.

Chapter 10

'There she is.' I whispered when I spotted Nameless seated on Queen Olosinwe's throne. Her hair was no longer in a ponytail, but let loose and seating on her head was also Queen Olosinwe's crown. She had also changed her pervious outfit, now she was wearing only white wrappas, one tied around her chest and another around her waist to form a knee length skirt.

'Stop her. I will rally my people, so they can be safe and I will also distract the guards as best as I can. I must leave you now. I hope we meet after this battle.' Queen Olosinwe said in farewell and left us alone.

Drumming began, Chief Izinwa was standing in front of the throne facing the people, he looked like he was sprung tight and the displeasure on his face was very clear, but so was his fear.

'People of Ulogboro. Today, we are here to celebrate a new queen. A queen of darkness, a queen with the strength and power of demons. We are here to celebrate her and watch her become one with her husband-to-be.' he said to the crowd who remained silent.

Nameless didn't care about the people, she smirked and sat up, waiting for whoever her future husband was to appear before the crowd.

'Who is the husband-to-be?' Mike asked, but it was a silly question, since we had all been kept in captivity together.

'Now, the procession of the soon-to-be king.' Chief Izinwa said and two guards dragged a struggling person with a sack on his head towards Nameless. Once they were in front of her, the guards let go of the person and roughly removed the sack.

It was Zina and he looked terrible. He had bruises on his arms and a few on his face. Nameless watched him, without any emotion, taking in his appearance before a wicked smile formed and she shouted.

'Behold, my one and only. I have waited for this day to come and now I have been blessed. King Dauda shall return and we shall rule beyond the land.'

Zina started struggling once again, but it was pointless, the guards were stronger than him and so was Nameless.

'Annabelle, she's going to get her husband back by making Zina his host!' Mike said with so much anger, he was vibrating. We had to stop her. I was also angry, it was time this carnage was over, Nameless was causing too much hurt and destruction and she had killed innocent people.

I encouraged my anger and I started growing, I grew so big, I didn't have to move to grab her and trap her tight within my fisted palm, the site of my gigantic form had everyone freezing. I looked at my friends and shouted 'Free Zina and let's free these people.'

I looked at Nameless, but instead of being met by an angry Zoe, she was limp in my arm, as if Nameless had fallen asleep or fainted. Something wasn't right.

I looked around and was surprised at how far my friends had come. Mara was handling three guards by herself. Mike ran his swords through anything that was in his way and when I was worried I couldn't find Nodebe I noticed a shadow pass over me and when I looked up, I saw Nodebe on the back of a Serpent? It looked almost like Nife except instead of blue, it had green skin.

While I was surveying my surrounding, I took a hard hit from behind and went crashing to the ground, flattening anything that was below me. I checked on Zoe and, saw she was still unconscious. I looked for what had attacked me, when I saw a scary looking giant Serpent with red and white scales, the eyes of the snake were glowing blood red. This serpent was different from the rest because it had a long snout, with big and dangerous looking canines, whatever was coming out of its mouth was acidic because one drop of the liquid made a smoking hole in the ground.

'It's over Geantoa. This is the end! I will rule. Ezyron will rise! Chaos will always prevail.' The Serpent hissed at me and, I knew immediately why Zoe's body was unconscious, Nameless had left it and transformed into this scary monster.

I spied Zina and I carefully dropped Zoe into his outstretched arms.

'Nameless, you've been given many opportunities to stop your reign of terror. But no more opportunities will be spared on something as evil as you. Fight me!' I screamed at her, knowing my friends were now somewhat safe.

'Never!' Nameless hissed back at me and spat her acidic venom at me, but I easily moved out of its way.

Something about her seemed familiar, like I should know about her. She launched herself at me, but I was ready and when she was close enough, I used my sword to strike out and it went through her hide, but instead of blood, hot smoke rushed out through the wound.

She let out a terrified hiss and recoiled.

'Mummy! Mummy!' I screamed as I ran as fast as my little legs could carry me.

My mummy was the only one around, my daddy had travelled the day before, I thought she would be asleep but the lights in the room were on and my mum was upright on the bed and inhaling the smoke from a bowl of something hot, she didn't mind the smoke was clouding her face.

She looked so tired, and ill. I began to cry, because I knew something was wrong. Which startled her, because she looked at me with surprise before she lightly scolded me. 'Annie, what's wrong? You're supposed to be in bed.'

She beckoned me to join her on the bed, and when I was settled beside her and I felt safe, I said 'Mummy, the scary thing came back again. It was worse than before, but I couldn't see the face properly. All I saw was eight red glowing eyes.'

I had never gone into details about my dream, but none of them had been this vivid or scary, I looked up at my mummy and she looked sicker, and even a bit worried.

'Oh Annie…it's just a nightmare but don't forget to always pray, now how about a story, huh?' she said, and hugged me.

I knew she was going to say it was a nightmare and would offer to tell me a story, she always did so. 'But Mummy, you said that every dream has a meaning. Does that mean that something bad is going to happen to me?' I asked not wanting to believe my dream didn't mean anything.

My mum closed her eyes for a bit as if she wanted to cry and when she opened her eyes, her turquoise eyes looked very clear. 'Annie, you're thinking way too much for a six year old. You need to sleep and I know a story that will make you sleep but also teach you a lesson.'

This was her way of telling me to drop something, so I did 'Okay.' I said and laid my head against her chest. My mum smiled and began to stroke my short brown hair.

'Once upon a time, there was a snake charmer, a beautiful lady with long black hair as dark as the night and skin as brown as the earth. She was the finest creation of Rinesie, the god of snakes. She was a hero among the people, because she would save them from the terror that was the great snake, Babo. The mistake.

One day, she was with Rinesie, who had left her alone to get a gift, but she did not respect his privacy, because she began to snoop around, and went through Rinesie's things. She came across a beautiful golden whistle with a purple snake made out of a shiny gem curled around it. She decided to take it and kept it in her pocket.

She left Rinesie home, and returned back to hers, where she used her new stolen treasure to charm snakes and when that wasn't enough she moved to charming people, which she did so well she became their Queen. She rose and became very powerful, to the point at which she felt invincible, which was a mistake because Rinesie had been watching her the whole time.

One day, she was taking a walk through her kingdom, when she saw a young blacksmith who she fell hopelessly in love with, the blacksmith remained with her not out of love but fear. She found out and casted a spell on him, so he would lose his fear and love her completely.

They got married not long after and on their wedding night, while they laid in bed, a powerful beam of light lit up the whole room and when she looked she saw her husband was on fire, but he was not in pain, because he was smiling.'

'Smiling?' I asked, interrupting my mother, who gave me a stern look, I hugged her and said a sorry for interrupting, so she continued speaking.

'She cried out, and asked him what he was doing but he let out a mocking laugh. He attacked her, by shooting flames from his left hand, which she narrowly escaped. She didn't understand, her husband was a mere mortal, he

couldn't do any of this things, when she heard the words 'The subject cannot surpass its master.' In the familiar voice of Rinesie.

As soon as she had registered the words, she burst into flames, but the flames didn't kill her, instead it dried up her blood leaving her lifeless and white. The young man engulfed in flames looked up at the sky and asked.

'Uncle, shall I finish the job?'

He wasn't a mere mortal after all, but the son of Resoraa, the Sun King, brother of Rinesie. Rinesie wanted her to suffer more, so he told his nephew to fill her up with smoke. After that, Rinesie commanded her to become a giant snake, but he left her with her heart the only thing which had any sort of life form.

She ran away defeated, never to be seen again. Her name was Tafrikae but when he had burnt the life out of her, he had also taken her name.' my mum said and yawned, but everything had a name, so I had asked.

'What is she called now?'

'Nameless'

Nameless was the snake charmer, Tafrikae! I knew how to defeat her. I had to strike her heart. 'Greed is very bad. You were the best creation of Rinesie, yet you threw that all away for nothing, Nameless or should I say Tafrikae?' I shouted, knowing it would throw her off balance.

She stopped and hissed! 'How do you know my despicable name?' Nameless hissed out, wasn't it public knowledge?

'Don't worry about me, worry about yourself!' I shouted. That was all the distraction I needed, I threw myself at her chest, where I knew her heart was and with all my might, I thrusted my sword, through her hide and I felt it slice through her heart.

The effect was instant, she stopped moving and shrieking, and her carcass fell lifeless to the ground. The chaos had stopped and the remaining guards that were still alive where now standing mindlessly.

I was about to make myself smaller, when Nameless carcass started smoking until the whole body was surrounded by the thick black smoke, which was there one minute and was gone the next. Where the snake had laid was now an unconscious young lady with dark hair with earth brown skin, dressed in a red tube and wrapper.

I took a calming breathe and shrunk back to my average height and approached the woman, wielding my sword. She stirred and her golden eyes opened, she looked around confused, until her gaze fell upon me. Her eyes widened in recognition and her face contorted, the hatred she had for me adamantly displayed.

'You! You stabbed me!' she shouted moving to rise up, but her legs gave out and she went back down.

'What the—' she said in confusion, looking down and gasping when she saw her legs. She started examining her body, and was surprised to feel her flesh.

'How did you do this?' she asked out, and started trembling.

'If you had been completely evil Tafrikae, you would have died, but you're not and here we are.' I said.

'Seize her!'

I heard Queen Olosinwe scream and was running with her guards towards where Tafrikae and I stood. When they got to us, two guards seized Tafrikae and Queen Olosinwe addressed her.

'It's finally time for you to pay for all that you have done to this kingdom, Nameless.'

'Queen Olosinwe, please you—' I interrupted her, but she wasn't listening.

'Thank you Annabelle for helping us. I will take it from here. My maidens will assist you and your friends, so you can freshen up and wear fresh clothes as well as eat and stock up on food.'

'But Queen Olo—'

'Also, if you want some horses and more weapons we can—'

'You can't take Nameless!' I shouted finally, out of frustration.

Queen Olosinwe looked at me confused.

'Why not?' she asked.

'Nameless, was cursed. She wanted nothing more than to be free of her curse, even though she chose destruction. It wasn't her doing she was purposely filled with hate and brainwashed. Although she is a selfish and greedy person, who takes what isn't hers. I need her to defeat Ezyron, she's the only chance I have and why I have spared her life.'

I said, hoping Queen Olosinwe would heed to my wish. She remained quiet and took on the pose of someone who was deep in thought, when she finally sighed and said.

'Annabelle, this is hard for me. This woman, has made me and my people suffer. She killed my husband, she has to pay for her crimes, because I know she can remember all that she has done. If you take her, you must return her to face trial.'

Queen Olosinwe said in a tone that brokered no argument, which was all I needed.

• • •

'Thank you once again Queen Olosinwe.' I said, carrying the backpack Queen Olosinwe's weavers had made for me. We were all properly fed, nourished and healed, thanks to Kion's flask which contained the healing drink, I was able to recover it, from beside the hut we had been hiding at first. The native healers also helped, with all the concoctions and paste they had made from herbs, which had been slobbered all over our wounds.

The tailors of Ulogboro were something else, because they had managed to sew outfits for us, we all had new shorts and shirts, which had been embroidered with their gold symbols. At least we had brought about new clothing styles for the villagers.

'It represents power and honour. This is one of our ways of showing our thankfulness.' Queen Olosinwe said quietly, when she caught me staring at the signs.

'We have to go now. The map says we have one more stop and we have less than a day.' Mara said examining the map, but that couldn't be right.

I took the map from her, but on the village was an X, which meant the gem had to be here somewhere.

'It can't be.'

'What can't be?' Tafrikae asked, but when I looked at her, I saw what I was looking for. The gem. An emerald gem, was on her forehead, just like the gem that had been on the whistle, in my mum's story.

'Tafrikae, don't move.' I said and approached her, gently I removed the gem from her forehead, which surprised her, because it had not been there before. She reached up and started feeling her forehead, when she cried out.

'Is there a dent? Please tell me there is no dent on my pretty head.'

She was such a drama queen, but Zoe shut her. 'Too bad your forehead is fine. I wish there was a dent.'

While they bickered the gem sank into my hand as usual.

'Okay, so three gems now. One to go, let's get moving people!' I shouted, before whistling for Nife, I felt the strong wind, before I even saw her, and she gracefully landed before me.

'Good girl.' I said as I stroked her head. 'Nife, carriage!'

The carriage appeared and Zoe started to climb up and unto it, when Zina stopped and looked around. Nodebe was missing.

'Where did that little rascal Nodebe run off to now?' He asked in frustration, looking around, hoping to spot his brother hiding somewhere.

We didn't have to guess long, because the dragon from the battle flew into the clearing and landed before us. On top of it was Nodebe, who had a look of pleasure and self-satisfaction on his face.

'Nodebe, where did this dragon come from?' I asked apprehensively.

'It came from the book. It's very useful.' Nodebe said, patting the beast, which was glaring down at us.

'Noddy, it seems dangerous.' Mara said, taking a few steps back.

'Yes it is, but don't worry, it listens to me. Let's go!' he said excitedly, ignoring the scared looks of everyone around him. The others looked at me for assurance and I sighed.

'I don't want Nodebe on that thing alone, so I'll go with him.' Zina said breaking our silence.

'I'll go with you to.' Mike piped up, and it was decided, they would follow behind us.

I didn't try to deter them or convince Nodebe to get down, because he wouldn't and time would have been wasted.

It wasn't on purpose but the boys had divided from us girls, I knew being trapped in a small space with Zoe and Tafrikae would be disastrous, but they had no choice and I hoped they behaved themselves.

The carriage remained quiet, each girl taking a corner and not interacting with one another. Which was fine by me, it had been a while since I had peace and quiet, not long into the flight, Mara fell asleep and I wished I could also, but it was time for me to question Tafrikae.

'Tafrikae, what should we know about Ezyron?' I asked.

'Ezyron? Everyone knows he is a cheat, liar and an egomaniac. That's what got him trapped in the first place.' Tafrikae said.

'How did he get trapped?' I questioned her.

Tafrikae sighed and stared at nothing in particular, with a solemn look of regret on her face, before she started speaking.

'I used to be involved with Ezyron. Ezyron was in the human form of a male, bedazzled me with his powers, and I wanted him to teach me, even though I had my own powers. I was always hungry for more power, at least back then. In the process I fell for him, and was blinded by his power and my greed. He was using me, because I didn't know I was helping him destroy the other gods so he could rule. With my powers I helped him deceive the gods of the four elements.'

'One day, I confessed how I felt for him, but he laughed at me and called me foolish. He then made me aware of all he had been doing and how I had been a blind accomplice, he could never love someone like me. I was heartbroken and I became weak and bitter.'

'In revenge, I informed the gods, who I had helped him deceive about what I had discovered. This led to them capturing him and sealing him, with their combined powers placed in four gems. After they had imprisoned him, the four gems had to be hidden in different locations, because together they were extremely powerful and would be dangerous in the hands of the wrong person. They knew a time would come when Ezyron would escape, so the prophecy was born, when the time would come, a Geantoa will save the day.'

It was a lot to take in, especially now that all the bits and pieces where now in place and I had a full picture of the history behind Ezyron, yet something was still bothering me.

'If Ezyron was captured? Why does he still have powers and many minions?' I asked, because how did my parents make deals with him? Why was my mother betrothed to him?

'Because, the Gods, didn't seal all of his powers and Ezyron is connected to all his followers, he doesn't need to be there to speak to them. He can be anywhere and command any of his followers to do his biddings, especially since he has granted them some sort of divinity spirit.'

I wouldn't forget to seal Ezyron's powers this time around, I would make sure Ezyron was forgotten and powerless even if it was the last thing I did.

Chapter 11

We had been at the abandoned castle, which the map had directed us to, for a while now, going through different rooms and walkways, which were badly infested with cobwebs and various plants which seemed to be growing all over the castle. Yet we had not encountered anything or seen anything that looked out of place.

'The next time I take a bath, I'll stay in for hours scrubbing this place off my body.' Mara said and her body shook in disgust.

'Are you sure we are in the right place?' Zoe questioned.

'Yes, the map led us here and—'

'This is the place. I remember it.' Tafrikae said, interrupting Mara.

'Doesn't matter, this is getting us nowhere.' Zoe complained, her frown was now a permanent fixture on her face.

'Are we going to find the final gem on time?' Nodebe asked the question I had been asking myself, after entering so many rooms with no result.

If we wanted to go through the castle at a faster pace, we had to split up. I didn't like the thought of us splitting up, but it was the best option and I was about to say so, when Mike spoke up.

'Let's break up. That way we can search faster.' Mike said, looking at me to see if his suggestion was okay with me. I nodded my head in approval and said.

'Let's do it. Pick a partner.'

'Mike!' Mara shouted and quickly grabbed his hand, which threw Mike off, he was surprised she had picked him.

'Fine but don't grip my arm or any part of me so tight, deal? He said.

'Of course.' Mara giggled.

I knew it! Mara had a crush on Mike, the way she had been hanging off him every chance she got, and she just giggled, it was so obvious. I was surprised Mike hadn't figured it out.

'I'll be on my own, thank you very much.' Tafrikae said and was about to run off, when I grabbed her arm and glared at her, did she think I was stupid?

'Oh no you don't. You stay with me always. This is not an opportunity for you to escape.'

I said firmly, which made her turn red in the face.

'Fine.' She said and rolled her eyes.

'I will go with Annabelle and Tafrikae.' Zina said, which left me and all the other girls shocked. Nodebe and Mike were looking everywhere but at Zina and Zoe.

'What?' Zoe shouted at him.

'You heard me Zoe.' Zina stated and crossed his arms in front of him, like he was ready to argue.

'You aren't being serious Zina.' Zoe said in a quiet voice, filled with hurt and then she clenched her fists.

'Zoe, stop, we've spoken about this.' He sighed, his eyes becoming tired as he stared at her.

'I will and Zina, we're done.' Zoe spat at him, she grabbed Nodebe's arm and marched away with Nodebe.

'She reminds me of me at times.' Tafrikae said, when we still hadn't moved long after Zoe had stormed away.

'Not helping. Okay, let's break up.' I said to Mike and Mara, before I and Tafrikae started walking after Zina who was already ahead on us.

• • •

'I don't think whatever it is you're looking for is in this castle.' Tafrikae said, we had just finished searching what seemed to be our twentieth room, together. Zina hadn't been searching the same rooms with us, it felt like he needed space so I let him be, even though I really wanted to check on him.

'Tafrikae, search that room and—'

"Don't try to escape. I got it.' Tafrikae rudely cut in, already heading for the room I had pointed to. I rolled my eyes at her retreating back.

I saw Tafrikae nod her head after taking a glance at Zina who was searching vigorously in another room. I sighed and went into the room that he was in.

I found Zina, surveying almost an empty room, and I timidly walked until I was standing beside him and said a quiet "Hi", which made him look up at my face.

'Hey.' He said, he smiled but it quickly dropped from his face, as if it hurt him so much, why had he and Zoe fought, what had he said to her, that had made her so upset? I liked Zina, and would like to be his girlfriend, but clearly he didn't so I had to be there for him as a friend.

'What happened with you two?' I asked.

'Because I couldn't keep deceiving her or myself.'

What was he talking about? Just at the start of this journey they were all loved up and looked like the world's happiest couple.

'At the start I really liked her, but my feelings faded away and I'm sure hers did also. We both knew it was over, especially when I fell for someone else. But she still didn't want us to break up, even though our relationship was pretty much over.'

Of course, there's another girl and Zoe being the spiteful person she was couldn't let another person win and I guess she wanted to be the one who broke up with him and in a public way. Zina would never notice me, wasn't it high time I gave up on him?

'Well now you're free I guess and you can go after who you really want.' I said trying my best not to let my disappointment show in my speech. I felt like crying, my chest was aching, and it really felt like my heart was being shredded to pieces.

'I really hope she likes me too. Annabelle, please look at me.'

Because of how desperate his pleading was, I looked at him and he was closer than he was before, his hand went to cup my cheek, he closed the space between our faces, when he pressed his lips against mine.

My heart felt like it was fighting its way out of my chest. Zina was kissing me. He kissed me. Was I the girl? I was the girl! He broke away from my lips and my hand went to feel my lip, it lasted mere seconds, but it was life changing seconds.

'Annabelle, I care about you. I have liked you for a while now and I'm not trying to rush you into anything. Oh my gosh. I'm sorry, I overstepped with kissing you. If you don't feel the same way I completely understand.'

He said and was rubbing the back of his head in a sheepish way.

I couldn't find my voice to tell him how I felt, I was finally about to speak when someone ran into the room and shut the door. Whoever it was had a hood covering his head, my heart started beating fast because the body looked familiar.

'Thank goodness.' The hooded person said and turned around.

'Annabelle?' Kion asked, his handsome smile spreading on his face, he started moving towards me and engulfed me in a warm hug. I was also happy to see him again.

'You know each other?' Zina asked, his jealousy clear in his voice.

'Yes. Kion, Zina. Zina, Kion.' I introduced them to each other.

'Nice to meet you! You must be one of her friends. I see you're doing well.' Kion said, extending his hand out to Zina, who took it but looked back at me with a questioning look on his face.

'Kion, what are you doing here?' I asked curiously, I really wasn't expecting to see him again.

'Sent here to protect the chosen one. Apparently, he's not dead. Crazy, right?' He said, which made me frown, why was he so sure the chosen one was male? Was it that he thought a female couldn't take down Ezyron? 'Are you still on that your mission?' he asked, when I remained quiet, he was now leaning against the door.

'He knows about Ezyron?' Zina asked in a hard voice.

'Yes I know about Ezyron, problem?' Kion asked, a mocking smile forming on his face.

Zina ignored him and asked me another question 'Annabelle, where did you meet him?' when he finished speaking, Zina moved to stand in front me.

'Zina, I'll tell you later. We really should be looking for the gem.' I said at last, the male testosterone in the room was intense and I needed air before they started beating their chests.

'Gem? Wait a minute! The chosen one is supposed to be looking for gems.' Kion said, looking at me, like he expected me to give him an answer.

'Kion, I am the chosen one you seek. A girl, not a boy like you are so set on it being. Me, Annabelle.' I said, crossing my arms in front of me. I felt proud. It was so typical male, to think a girl couldn't be a hero.

I had shocked Kion into silence and it felt really good, he even looked sorry and started speaking. 'Annie, I—'

'Annie?' Zina questioned, shocked at Kion's familiarity, he was starting to get on my nerves. I wasn't his girlfriend and some hours ago he had a girlfriend that wasn't me.

'There's no time for this. Let's go and search for the gem now!' I said, making them know how frustrated I was feeling, wasting precious time. I walked out of the room and entered another room, which was filled with different things and I immediately started searching through the items.

'What does it look like?' Kion asked, shifting through a heap of silver stacked at a corner of the room.

'A shiny transparent rock. It's somewhere in this castle.' I said.

'How would we know if it's the real gem?' Kion asked again.

'I would know, once I touch it. Oh my gosh where is it! Ezyron is rising in a few hours!' I shouted in frustration the drawers I was searching.

'Actually by sunset, which is two hours from now.' A voice I didn't recognize said, which made us all stop and look around.

A young man stepped out of the shadows, he looked to be in his thirties and was wearing a draped cloth held together at the waist with a golden rope. The most disturbing thing about this man were his eyes, he had no pupils.

'I've been waiting for you, dear Annabelle.' he said, which had my hackles rising. Finally some evil spirit sent by Ezyron had come, all I had to was defeat it and the gem would appear. I raised my sword and pointed it at him, taking a defensive stance, which Kion and Zina also took up.

'Who are you? Why have you been waiting for me?' I questioned him.

'I am Etayo. The god of peace. I'm here to help you search for the final gem.' When he had said his name, he had started glowing which was very odd to see, but if he was really a god, then I guess it would be expected.

'A god?' I questioned yet again.

'Yes. I am a god.'

'I didn't ask for any godly help.'

'You don't need to ask. I appear when I'm needed.' Etayo replied me, but if he was really a god that came when he was needed, why did he appear now and not when I was being attacked and was losing all my hope?

It seemed Etayo had read my thoughts because he said to me, a wry smile on his face. 'You always found a way before I could intervene.'

'Why? You don't need people, if Ezyron took over, you and all the other gods will be fine.'

'We gods live on through the worship of mortals. A god must be remembered in order to live, yes many people do not worship us gods, and have chosen to focus on just one god, which you all praise with a capital G, which is funny because he is one of us. Because of this, the rest of the gods are weakened while God thrives.' he said with so much bitterness for God.

'So you're only intervening for selfish reasons, of course.' I said, rolling my eyes.

'Doesn't matter now does it? I am here to help, besides I am only helping because you're more than a mere mortal, why do you think people like you are rare?' he said ignoring my scorn and a smirk started taking form on his face.

'My mum? She was a god?' I asked.

'Your mother, Angela Nijala Nguma, a very beautiful lady. It's sad that she's not here to see you. She would have been proud.' he said not answering my question, which frustrated me.

'That's not an answer! You are a servant of Ezyron.' I shouted at him and charged at him, ready to be done with him, but all he had to do was snap his fingers and I went crashing into a wall.

'Annabelle!' I heard the guys shout and their pounding footsteps as they ran to me. The crash had given me a headache and I was suddenly exhausted.

'I hate this god,' I growled at Zina and Kion, Zina crouched down and was checking on me, but I bathed his hands away, I was fine and he didn't need to fuss over me.

'I'll go talk to Etayo. He is a god and we have to show him power respect. You both should wait here.' Kion said.

Zina picked up a hand of mine, and held it in his, which made Kion stare at our joined hands for a few seconds before he returned to where Etayo, the fake god of peace was now lounging against a wall.

Kion prostrated before Etayo and greeted him with the words 'Greeting to the god who reigns peace upon the lands.' Etayo looked pleased that he was getting the respect he deserved.

'Finally, respect Kion Jayclen Xecleyha, I'm surprised you still do not recognise me with all that studying you do in that funny school of yours. But of course you never sacrificed any offering to me, even when I showed the Wollocks the way to you but being the nice person that I am, I only punish.'

'We are really sorry my lord. It's a mistake that won't repeat itself again. I also apologise for Annabelle's behaviour—'

The god sighed. 'I want her to succeed, because Ezyron must not rise again.' he said with a scowl.

'Annabelle, we have to find the gem now.' He said and ran to an overturned wardrobe, which he started searching vigorously.

'Kion, why the sudden rush?'

'What does your map say after this place?' he asked without glancing up.

I took out the map from my bag to look for out next and final location, but the castle seemed to be our final destination. I was about to tell Kion, it was a dead end, when the map burst into flames and I screamed as I let it go, I watched it quickly become ashes.

'Kion, what's going on?' Zina asked in a demanding tone.

'We have next to no time left, let's find it now!'

• • •

'Yes, yes, move faster. It's in here somewhere.' Etayo shouted, from his stone throne, which he had made out of thin air. I was about to tell him he wasn't helping by giving us commands when the castle shook dangerously and everything in the room became even more chaotic.

Just like it started, the quake stopped with no warning. Even though we were all unsettled Kion immediately went back to searching for the gem and even Etayo had now joined the search, and I had to blink several times because Etayo movements were as fast as lightning.

'Why are two of you acting so frenzied?' I shouted at them, they knew something and were keeping me out of the loop. I needed to know it and now.

'If Ezyron rises, I will merge with him. I won't live that life again.' Etayo whined.

'Merge with him? You're after all his minion!' I said, growing angry because I had been right all along.

'No! Etayo is his twin brother and in all the stories Etayo and Ezyron, are one if they are in the same world. War needs peace to stop. That is why he doesn't want Ezyron to—'

'Kion, when you told me to check the map…' I trailed off, because dread instantly filled up my stomach as I came to a scary realization.

'Uh-huh!' Kion said, knowing what I had discovered. 'There's no other place after this castle.'

Kion finished speaking for me, for the benefit of Zina.

'We are standing above Ezyron's Tomb. The battle ends here.' Kion said in a gravely tone.

I couldn't do it. No, I was not going to face a god, whose twin brother didn't even want. I was a thirteen-year-old. I was just dreaming and I would wake up. My mum, dad and brother would be a family, and they'll laugh at my crazy dream.

'I don't think I can do this!' I said and started pacing around the room.

'You're just nervous. Get it together! You are the chosen one for a reason. The world needs you. You, Annabelle Nguma. You have come a long way from the sheltered girl you were. You are a Geantoa and you're going to kick Ezyron's butt.'

Zina said encouragingly, he was pacing with me, but he pulled me into a hug, which was really helpful because it managed to calm me down. I opened my eyes and something twinkling caught my attention. It was the final gem and it was blue in colour, sapphire. I slowly extracted myself from the hug and walked towards the gem. Everyone in the room had paused when they saw me walk with determination and when I picked up the gem, they all let out a collective sigh of relief.

'We need to find the others and get to the tomb!' Zina excited said, but we weren't going to be doing that, because the ground gave and down we went.

Chapter 12

Zina, Kion and I yelled as we fell at an alarming speed to our death, but after seconds of screaming. I heard laughter and I opened my eyes, we were suspended a few feet from the ground and Etayo was laughing at us. Zina and Kion also stopped screaming and their eyes were wide open. Etayo noticing we had stopped screaming released us and we dropped gently to the ground.

'Welcome to my dear brother, Ezyron's tomb.' Etayo announced, while we stood and started dusting ourselves.

The room was enormous. The walls were covered with symbols, and then there was the door. It was painted red, and drawn on the sides of the door were two sets of eyes. But where an handle should have been were four empty holes.

'That's where the gems are meant to be.' Kion said noticing it as well.

'Why do those doors look familiar?' Zina asked, staring at it curiously.

'They look exactly like the one at the museum!' I exclaimed.

'They are portals from the mortal world to here.' Kion said, sounding like he was lost in thought

'Kion?' I asked and placed a hand on his shoulder.

He looked at me and smiled.

'I'm fine, how do we find the rest of your friends?' he asked.

'You need not bother, they are here already!' A loud voice boomed.

A door opened and Zoe, Mara, Mike and Nodebe filed into the room robot like. The gold on their outfits had turned red as well as their eyes which were now dark shades of red. No! This was my greatest fear come to pass for real now. Ezyron controlling my friends.

'No! Zoe fight it! Mike, Nodebe don't let him win! Mara please wake up!' I shouted.

'Ah child! They cannot hear you! Minions kill her!' Ezyron commanded my friends, who immediately advanced with the lions which appeared out of nothing.

I pulled out my sword and looked at Kion and Zina who were standing beside me, their swords also drawn.

'We can't hurt them.' Zina said, his gaze worried.

'We can't, we need to wake them up, if not let's knock them out. Etayo, you're a god, what do we do?' I asked, looking at the god, who was sitting in a corner looking bored.'

'He's using Lachaise, he is controlling their spirits.'

'How is that helpful?'

'It isn't. You wanted to know something and I gave you something. What to do? I can't help you. It's your mission not mine.' he said and closed his eyes.

• • •

It turns out that Lachaise did not only allow Ezyron control people, it also gave them unnatural strength. I was up against Zoe, which was a bad move on my path. She kept firing her deadly arrow after arrow with unnatural speed, which made it a very tasking job avoiding them.

I got close enough to strike her with the hilt of my sword and she immediately went down. Before I could move one, I realized she was only pretending, using her feet she kicked mine and I went crashing to the ground. She jumped on me throwing punches on stomach, before she dragged me up and flung me away like I was a jacket. The whole room shook when I crashed into a wall and I lost consciousness for a few seconds.

When I came to and opened my eyes, I was met with horror. Zina was on the ground and Mike had his sword pointed at his neck, which Zina was trying to escape from. Kion was underneath Mara who was pummelling him and an arrow end was sticking out of his shoulder.

Ezyron scornful laughter filled the room, because he was clearly winning. I searched for Etayo and saw he was battling the lions, which was strange to see, because the lions were losing against him. But where was Nodebe?

I got my answer immediately as another hidden door exploded and a strange creature crashed into the room. The top half of the creature was that of a gorilla, it was gigantic and its massive arms looked even more dangerous. The lower half belonged to a scorpion, it's dangerous tip was flicking left to right looking for someone to sting. When the black beady eyes landed on me, it started beating its chest with its fist, before it let out a deafening and ground shaking roar.

It leaped and I scrambled out of the way in time for it to crash into the wall, which began a game of cat and mouse, where I avoid the creature at sharp corners, which had it slamming into the walls, after a couple of continuous crashing, the final crash knocked it out.

I had to help my friends. I ran towards where Zina and Mike were battling, from the corner of my eye I saw Zoe running for me. She jumped ready to take me down, but I was ready for her. I ducked and grabbed her ankle, and with all my might I swung her towards a wall.

I tackled Mike and got him away from Zina. I was on top of him, I tried to punch him in the face to knock him out, but he held both my hands and used his leg to kick me and I went crashing into a wall. I was really starting to hate walls.

My head was aching as well as my whole body. The pain I felt was total agony. I knew I wouldn't be able to get up and it was starting to fade out, I helplessly watched my friends fighting against each other, and Nodebe was reading from the book, his eyes were gold and were glowing brightly, it felt like Ezyron had gotten what he wanted.

'Yes! I am about to rise Nguma. I can't wait to take your life and be paid my debt. Your world will never be the same.'

I looked at the door that had trapped Ezyron all these years, and I felt like a failure, I had failed and doomed everyone. The door was opening and shadows began seeping out of the door.

I couldn't give up now, Ezyron couldn't win, I wasn't weak and helpless. One look around the room and seeing my friends hurting one another made me so frustrated and angry. I clenched my fists, the hilt of my sword digging into my palm and embraced my anger, which made me start growing and I did not stop growing until I was bigger than the beast. The beast had risen again and was now headed my way, I was ready for it, I was ready to be done with Ezyron.

It leaped but I caught it mid-air and punched it hard in the face, before slamming it on the ground, stepping and holding down its tail, so it wouldn't sting me and without hesitating I sliced off the head of the beast and it disintegrated into nothing.

and I pushed my hair back feeling my body glazed with sweat. My eyes caught Zina and Zoe who were at each other's throats. I marched towards them and picked up Zoe, before slamming her against the wall, levelling her to my face and screamed at her.

'Zoe! If you can hear me, you have to fight it!' It didn't reach her, because all she did was laugh.

'Child. You are so gullible and naïve. Nothing can stop me.' Ezyron said through her.

'Not on my watch.' I muttered, and I focused my mind to feel and bring forth water.

The water is my strength.

I used the water to hold Zoe back, I ran over to the door sealing Ezyron and closed it, urging the gems to show themselves and out they came red, yellow, green, and blue, warm against my palm. I hurriedly placed the gems into the slots on the door and when I had gotten to putting the last and final gem, the blue one. It was too late.

The door opened with a powerful blast that sent me backwards and had me falling to the ground. I watched in horror as a twenty feet giant with bright red glowing eyes and white glistening teeth stepped into the room, it's evil eyes focused on me.

Ezyron had finally risen.

Chapter 13

Ezyron appeared in the gigantic form of a human man. A smirk on his devilishly face, he was beautiful yet scary at the same time. He had on only his trouser shorts, his chest was wide, hairy and muscular. He had muscles everywhere which made me gulp, especially when he bent down to look at my frozen sprawled form on the floor.

'Ah, just as beautiful as her mother.' he said, a devious smile forming on his face, when he reached out a finger and caressed my cheek. I was too shocked to even bat away his finger, when his finger went to my hair, I was released from my spell and I shook his hand off which made him laugh.

'Don't be a foolish child, I have risen. Your family has wronged me and I shall take my revenge, unless you join me and become my bride, if not I'll have no choice but to kill you.'

My temperature had risen with each word that had left his mouth and when I tried to move my arms it felt impossible, I was paralyzed. He was going to hurt my family, no he was going to kill them.

'Join me, everything you love is gone.' He said and gestured towards my friends, who had all gotten quiet. They all were lying unmoving on the ground, it was worse than my greatest fear, seeing them looking lifeless.

I let out a scream filled with anguish, which had Ezyron laughing and I badly wished I could move so I could shove my sword through his neck and chop off his head.

'Calm down, they aren't dead yet, but they soon will be, once I am through with you!'

'Never!' I shouted back at him.

Ezyron does not want to kill me for a debt.

He is afraid of me because I can end his rising.

I should not be afraid of him.

I am fighting for my family and friends.

I am fighting for the world.

'I choose death, but I doubt that it would be my fate.' I said, I felt life in my arms again and I knew I could move. I reached out my finger and pushed him hard in between the eyes.

He shrieked as he fell backwards, with my connection to water, I called on a torrent, which I used to hold him down.

'This fight won't be easy!' He shouted at me, before he struggled out of the hold. I looked at his hand pressed flatly against the ground. I knew nothing good would come of it and I was right a mass of shadows coming from a corner of the room started seeping into him from the tips of his fingers, and when I looked to see what was fuelling him, I couldn't help but scream.

It was Etayo's essence, what Etayo had feared was coming to pass and I knew Ezyron would be ten times stronger now, when he finished merging Etayo to him. He cackled, his skin turning as black as coal and he further increased in size with his muscles bulging. His black mass of hair set ablaze and became a huge mane of fire atop his head.

Ezyron was now larger than life. It was surprising how the room hadn't crumbled because of the sheer size of him. It was alarming how the room seemed to have also expanded to accommodate the giant.

He stood to his full height and opened his eyelids, I almost wet myself, because of his eyes. They were no longer just a set of red glowing eyes, he now had two pairs. Four glowing red eyes.

'One last chance Geantoa!' he shouted at me and when I refused to yield, his fist moved at the speed of lightning, punched me in the face, sending me across the room. Before I could get up or think to retaliate, Ezyron picked me up by my neck and threw me again to the other side of the room. I couldn't prepare myself for the impact and I groaned in serious pain.

I couldn't win this battle, by myself.

I pressed my hand against the ground, hoping to use water against him but before the water reached him, he stomped his foot hard against the ground causing a minor earthquake, which caused glowing red cracks to appear on the ground, and the water to disappear.

'We are above the dark world. I will send you to your worst nightmare. It is no place for a Geantoa.' He said, hurling discarded stone after stone at me.

The stones exploded every time they collided with the wall where I had been a few seconds ago, I dodged each and every one of his throws. When he grew tired, he grabbed me by the throat and strangled me. I struggled to pry his hand off, but it was no use. I was starting to see black spots, my head got woozy from no air and my struggling was slowly becoming weaker.

'The world will bow down to me I shall never be forgotten.' he said, letting the final words I ever hear be his gloating victory. But Ezyron's hand released its hold, and I started coughing as I struggled to take in the air. My upper body was covered in blood, and at my feet was the hand Ezyron had been using to strangle me.

Ezyron was screaming in agony, but I couldn't focus on him just yet, still panting for air, I looked around the room for my saviour when I saw them. A young creature, with orange skin and hair that was ablaze stood beside Tafrikae.

'Why do the ugly ones always come back?' Tafrikae said, not masking the spite in her voice, when Kiola started shooting Ezyron in the face with fire from her palms.

Ezyron growled when the fire touched him, but I really could not tell if the fire had burnt him or not.

'Ah my love. I thought I would never see you again. Why help the child? Why not join me and secure your future? I have missed you.' He said, to Tafrikae, who looked conflicted, she still had feelings for him.

'Tafrikae, don't listen to him! He's only deceiving you. He doesn't care about anyone!' I shouted.

'You Geantoas and your big mouths.' Ezyron huffed out in annoyance and threw a fireball at me.

I was too weak to move, from being deprived of air for so long, so I shut my eyes and waited for the impact, I knew it wouldn't kill me, when, I felt a gush of wind slap my face and before I knew it, I was moved out of the way. I looked at her orange face, she looked a bit pale, her orange-flaming hair was sticking out, and her dress was worn out, like it had been through the trails of time. Even though she had just saved me, I was still conflicted about whether to hug her or punch her in the face.

'Is Geantoa okay?' she asked meekly.

I felt a growl muster in my throat. I was tilting more to the latter. 'Yeah, thanks.' I mumbled and pushed her aside to go to Tafrikae, when she grabbed my hand, holding on to it firmly.

'I know Geantoa is angry with me. She believes that I betrayed her. Kiola is bad, yes but not a backstabber. I found your fellow Geantoa to save you. I cannot fight your friends lest I hurt them and Geantoa will never forgive me. I wanted to help but I was afraid. Kiola is not stable, and I do not want to be bad again. Please forgive me.' She said with a shaky voice. Her small eyes welled up with tears, and I put a finger on her shoulder.

'Kiola, I'm angry with you ever since you left. You're right. You said it yourself, you're unstable. I'm sorry but I can't trust you anymore.' I said, hoping my face was showing how serious I was.

'I understand but Kiola promises to gain Geantoa's trust no matter what even if Kiola dies.' She said softly.

'Come on, we have a world to save,' I said, giving her a small smile.

I looked up and saw Tafrikae shooting flames at Ezyron, while dodging his fast. I took my opening when I saw he was distracted, I willed a wave of water to slam into him. It knocked him off balance, and he went slamming unto the ground. The ground began to tremble.

'This is unacceptable.' Ezyron yelled as he got up.

'How do we stop him?' I said to Tafrikae as I ran up to her with Kiola by my side. I wasn't a giant anymore, I had shrunk the minute I started breathing again. Tafrikae looked at me from the corner of her eye, as she kept on firing at Ezyron. I decided to follow suit and hurl water balls at Ezyron.

'You'll have to separate him from his brother first then somehow subdue him and push him into his tomb. That way you can seal him for good with the stones. You have them right?' Tafrikae replied.

'Yeah but how do I separate him from Etayo?' I said weakly. I was in so much pain, I had to drop one hand and use only one to shoot.

'I'm sorry Annabelle, but that is for you to figure out. Duck!' she said and we managed to dodge Ezyron massive fist.

Tafrikae and I ran between Ezyron's legs and I stabbed him in the calf. He yelped in pain and I did the same thing to his other calf. Kiola transformed into a bird and was trying to scratch out Ezyron's eyes, when Ezyron slapped her away and she crashed into one of the many ruined walls.

'Kiola! I screamed and made a large cut on his calf.

'Arrrrrrggghhhh! Enough!' He yelled and slammed his fist against the ground making so many cracks that the room started to collapse on us, Tafrikae and I were stuck. Only my neck upwards was free from harm. No matter what we did, Tafrikae and my efforts were useless.

'Enough of this! The end is now! I am ending this once and for all!' he shouted and let out a loud growl as his fist slammed on me.

Chapter 19

I struggled to open my eyes and when I finally did, I was in a brightly lit space, that was completely white, like an endless white void.

Was I dead? I tried screaming, but no sound came out. I looked down at my body, which was completely healed and scar less, I was dressed in a simple short white gown and I couldn't feel pain. I looked down, startled when I saw a puddle of water start to appear at my feet, it stopped growing when I could see my full reflection in it.

My hair had been transformed and was plaited into messy French braids that came all the way to my chest, which was adorned with flower petals, which had different colours gold, sapphire and silver. I lifted an arm to touch one of the petals when I noticed there were some symbols on the inside of my arms running down in a straight line.

I was surprised at how innocent and pretty I actually looked, I had never thought of myself as beautiful, until now.

'Which isn't good because if you don't believe it, how do you expect others to believe as well?'

A soft female voice asked and I turned around quickly. A woman with skin, the colour of thick delicious honey and eyes so blue and mysterious, who was also wearing the same attire I was wearing, said from beside me.

'Who are you? Where am I?' I asked taking a step away. She seemed nice, but I could never be too sure these days.

'I am Esmirinim, the goddess of rivers.' She said and bowed at me.

'Aren't there many goddesses and gods of rivers?' I asked her.

'Yes, but I am of a major river, which makes me more important.' She replied.

I knew I had to be careful, about how I spoke to a god, even though I had found that they were all very cocky beings.

 'Okay, where am I?' I asked

'Asylum.' She said.

'Huh?' I asked, not sure that I got her right.

'You heard me, asylum. Do not worry child. You are not dead, but it doesn't mean that you are not on the verge of it. I managed to save your soul before he crushed you.'

I knew what she was talking about, so it hadn't been a dream.

'What's happening to me, if I'm not dead?' I said.

'Like I said, you're on the verge of death.'

'What am I going to do? The war is already lost,' I said defeatedly.

'Come here child,' Esmirinim said, and I reluctantly went. She held me by the shoulder and bent down, until she was at my eye level.

'Annabelle, you are a smart, beautiful and brave girl. You have heart and soul. Do you want to know why the prophecy chose you? It's because of how determined you are. You had the opportunity to run away from this and act like it never happened but you didn't. I will not tell you that life would be better if you survive this, but I can assure you that you have a bright destiny ahead of you, if you do. You shall always be remembered.' She said and brushed a piece of my stray hair out of my face.

I smiled at her, grateful for the words.

'But how do I stop Ezyron? I know I meant to separate him from Etayo but how?'

'That, my child, is for you to figure out, and you better be quick. Time is running out.' I groaned. 'I wish my mum was here.' I said absentmindedly.

'She is with you.' Esmirinim said and sighed. 'The heart is what we must follow. It is the answer to many problems.' She said, and by the time I looked up, she was gone.

'Esmirinim?' I called out but there was no response.

What do I do now?

I looked around trying to figure out a way of escape when I noticed my body was disintegrating.

• • •

I came through and grabbed Ezyron's fist before it collided with my body, it was very hard because I had broken bones and bruises all over my body.

'It's over kid. Your friends have seconds left to live and I got your rescue team,' he said, showing me Tafrikae and Kiola, who were now lifeless on the ground, just like my friends.

'Oh and before I destroy you, I just wanted to let you know that as we speak, I have your family in custody. I made a huge mistake making that stupid deal with your mother, but I will fix it by eliminating all of you.' he cackled after his speech.

I had been trying to protect them and now he had them. I felt my eyes start glowing, anger like I had never felt, had started brewing within me and I knew Ezyron was going to pay.

The water is your strength. The voice that always reminded me of my strength said but this time I recognized whose voice it was, my mum.

'Do not underestimate the water.' I said to Ezyron and pushed his fist away with such force he crashed into a wall. 'Water can be calm,' I said taking a deep breath before I continued 'But it is also deadly.' I said, I had reached his disoriented form on the floor now and I punched him in the face. I punched his face repeatedly, I was unhinged. I stopped to create a huge water ball from the ground and threw it at his chest, the water was so much he was drowning in it.

'It is also very sharp.' I started forming a sharp sword made of water, when the water from my previous blast let up and Ezyron opened his eyes, worry settled in his gaze, when he spotted the eight foot long, water sword, which hilt was decorated with sapphires and emeralds.

'Not that, not that, noooo...' He screamed, struggling to stand up, but failing woefully. I used my leg to slam him down and pin his chest.

'Water is like blood, it courses through the heart.' I said and raised the sword over his heart, I moved my leg to hold him down by his stomach and yelled 'Because, the heart of the ocean is the most powerful of them all.' Bringing the sword down and into his heart, it made a cracking sound and when I withdrew the sword, two gods flew apart.

I wasted no time. I pointed my sword at Ezyron who was trying to stand while holding his side, with his only hand, I formed a protective bubble with him in it and directed it through the red doors, Ezyron was struggling with all his might, but the bubble wouldn't give.

Once he was behind the doors, I ran and slammed the door shut.

'Come on,' I whispered, summoning the jewels, which came to my palms instantly and I put in the red gem, which transformed to white, which it hadn't done the first time, the yellow gem, and the green. I was ready to pass out, but I knew I needed to put the blue one too. The door was starting to open again, when I finally put the blue gem in.

I stepped back and watched all the gems began to glow, the light was blinding, which made me trip and fall to the ground. I was completely exhausted, the pain I was feeling was unbelievable and my vision started going blurry, the last thing I saw was a blurry black figure, which had me screaming 'Etayo! Help!'

Chapter 15

I slowly opened my eyes, and when they adjusted to the light I was in a hospital room. There was only one window in the room, a cabinet and table beside me with two red plastic chairs. I saw many wires plugged into me from a machine, and I somehow managed to make myself sit up, which was a painful ordeal. The handle of the door turned down and I smiled when my two favourite people in the world walked in.

'Cupcake!' My dad shouted, rushing to embrace me in a hug.

'I missed you so much Dad,' I cried and rested my head on his shoulder.

'I guess Andrew became invisible.' My brother said, and I let go of my dad, who moved out of the way so Andrew could hug me too.

'How you doing?' Andrew said, grabbing my hand, and rubbing a thumb soothingly on the back.

'I'm feeling better, but what about you? Are you okay? Did our stepfamily hurt you?' I asked them with concern, remembering what Ezyron had said about capturing them.

Dad looked at me sadly, before he looked away. I glanced at Andrew, but he was smiling at Dad.

'First, they kept us as prisoners. Later, they forced us to carry on with our lives by using a spell to watch our every move. They tortured us when we disobeyed them and mocked us whenever we sang of our faith in you. It was hard to believe that Onye was my wife.' Dad finally spoke out.

'I regret ever meeting that woman.' Dad said bitterly, I watched tears escape from his eyes, and I wished I destroyed my stepmother like I had destroyed Ezyron.

'How did you even meet her?' I asked, trying to control my anger. Andrew noticed, grabbed my hand, and gave it a gentle squeeze.

A squeeze I appreciated.

'I met her at a friend's party, three years after your mother died. She was nice to talk to and we had being single parents in common. We began to see each other more, and I am not sure if it was love, but something kept drawing me to her. Eventually, I married her and well, you know the rest. I remember the first time I invited her for a dinner, you ran away the moment you laid eyes on her. I should have seen it as a sign, but I was blind.'

I looked away as Dad said this. The first time I saw my step mum, I knew something was wrong about her, but I just did not know what. I grabbed my dad's hand.

'It's okay Dad. We all make mistakes. You were deceived and it is not your fault. You thought you could find Mum in someone else and hopefully, you will find that person because I know that Mum would want you to be happy,' I said with a smile that Dad returned.

'So you guys just suffered with them until I sealed Ezyron?' I asked confused.

'What? You think we're cowards? You know you're not the only one with powers,' Andrew said with a grin.

'No way! Andrew! How come you never told me about your powers before I learned of mine?' I asked, giving him a light punch on the arm. Andrew laughed.

'I didn't want my little sister knowing I was a freak. Besides, it was never easy controlling the powers. Shrinking after growing from being angry, finding excuses for the broken pipes at school or even the toilet. Nothing was easy but Dad helped, so I managed.' He said with a shrug.

'I bet you didn't show them mercy.' I slyly asked my brother.

'You know me too well sis,' we laughed over that and I could not help but pull them in for a group hug.

'So when am I going home, to my bed? Ugh, now that I am back there's even school.' I said sadly, but Andrew laughed nervously and Dad said nothing. 'Why are you both being strange?' I asked looking from one to the other.

'Listen Cupcake, you can't go to your school anymore, it's no longer safe for you, especially with how aware you are now, you'll be able to sense spirits, and many of who won't take kindly to being discovered and hate Geantoas. You'll be transferring to a new one.' he said calmly.

'No Dad, please I can't handle a new school right now, what about my friends? I kicked Ezyron's butt, I can handle spirits and anything.' I begged, on the verge of crying.

'Sorry Cupcake, no negotiation, I should have taken you there in the first place. It's perfect for you and your mum wanted you there, she went there.' my dad said candidly.

'Really?' I asked and he nodded.

'It's a school for your kind, the Geantoas. It's the safest place for you. It's also a boarding school and you'll be there all round, learning everything about the world you live in and how to protect yourself. Because of your late start, the school will only let you go home during the summer break.' My dad said.

I felt crushed, my life had changed drastically, and here was my dad, changing it even more by sending me away, he couldn't even wait until I was out of the hospital to tell me, but it looked like it hurt him more than it hurt me.

'What about Andrew?' I asked, wiping my tears away.

'Andrew is almost done with school and can fend for himself for now. Your aura is stronger, and I have already registered Andrew in a special college in Ethiopia.'

'Ethiopia?' I asked, I could feel my eyes widening.

'I know it's far Annie, but I'll visit. I promise,' Andrew said, as he ruffled my hair. I smiled at him.

'Well, we better go but we will discuss with your doctor about you getting discharged.' My dad said and gave me another hug.

I was about to ask about my friends, because I didn't remember getting out of the forest, but as soon as my family opened the door to my room, my friends instantly filled up my room, which surprised me.

I was ambushed by lots of bodies hugging me, one after the other, which made me laugh, after they had checked to see I was okay, they all moved back and lingered around me.

'How are you?' Mara asked, as she hugged me.

'I'm great and I see you guys are good as well,' I said.

'Yeah, we were able to heal faster, thanks to Kion who put some healing potion in our food after we healed,' Mike said.

I smiled at Kion who stood behind my friends and returned my smile.

Zina came and sat down beside me on my bed and said 'I'm really glad you're okay Annie.'

It made me smile and I faced him when I replied him 'Me too.'

Kion decided to take the other side of my bed and sat down there, he crossed his finger and held it over me, which had me looking at him for an answer.

'To make sure you're not possessed.' he said and shrugged.

I shook my head, because it hadn't even crossed my mind, my friends filled me up on all that had occurred after I had sealed Ezyron and passed out. They had all come through, and with the help of Kion, I was carried and we were all taken back to my village, where my brother was called and my dad had come to get us.

I knew Zoe was in the room, but it seemed she was staying away from the rest of us, I looked at her and she was busying staring down at the screen of her phone, she looked miserable and alone.

'Hey Zoe?' She looked up surprised, she wasn't expecting me to talk to her?

'Not even a hug for a friend?' I asked and I spread my arms out for her, I knew she needed one more than anyone in the room. Zina got up from his spot, when Zoe slowly approached, but she hugged me, when she pulled back, she looked at me, on the brink of tears and said.

'Thank you.'

'For what?' I asked.

'For not giving up on me even when I was unnecessarily mean to you. Thanks for always being there for me.' she said and wiped a tear that had fallen.

'I'm changing schools. Can't be going to schools for mortals, not safe for me or you guys. I'll be going to a school for Geantoas now.'

I said in one breathe, because it was the best time to inform them of the change, since we were all gathered together. They asked some questions and I found out Kion was also at the school I would be going to, after Kion explained somethings to us, and how it was safer for me to be at the school, we all agreed it was the best option for me, even though it was still saddening.

'I'm also changing schools.' Zoe said after a while of us being quiet.

'Oh. Why are you changing schools?' I asked her.

'My parents. I'm going to an all girl's military school.' She said frowning, which I understood, all the stories I had heard about how military school functioned was very scary.

'Wow, Zoe. You'll be allowed to come visit us though?' Mara said, also frowning. Her two closest girlfriends were leaving her. I wish Zoe didn't have to go.

'I'll try.' Zoe said

Zina didn't say anything but he was frowning, I didn't know what to say to him. Nodebe piped up and spoke about how he had given the PRISONOMIA book to Kion. Nodebe and Zina had decided that it wasn't safe for Nodebe to hang on to the book and it should be given back to me, which Kion said he would when he was done studying it.

Not long after that, my friends left my room, and I was left to my thoughts. I was relieved, my thoughts returned back to my encounter with Esmirinim *"I will not tell you that life would be better if you survive this, but I can assure you that you have a bright destiny ahead of you, if you do"*. Her words were now imprinted in my head. My life was going to get tougher no doubt, but I was glad I had discovered who I really was.

• • •

After two weeks in the hospital, I was discharged. Better and stronger than ever. The name of our school was Spirit Clove Academy. The academy was a multinational corporation, with schools in every part of the world.

Only people like us, who had spirit blood in our veins, would ever find or see the school, a mortal would never find it, unless a spirit spawn, revealed it. The best part of the school according to Kion, was how the school accommodated all kind of spirits and magical creatures.

I went to the school two days after I was discharged from the hospital, my dad was really serious about keeping me safe and wanted me locked up behind the protective walls of the school.

Before Andrew and I had left the house, our dad had called me in to the house and had given me a small navy blue box. Inside the box was a necklace, with a sapphire seashell with green lines. It was my mum's necklace and it had made me cry, because I never thought I would see the necklace again, she used to wear it all the time, and I had thought it was buried with her.

'She made me promise that when you discovered who you were, to give it to you. It always protected her and she hopes it would protect you, in place of her.' my dad had said sadly. I had hugged him hard after that, and cried a bit.

Dad wasn't following us to the school, he said it was better if he didn't know the way to it yet, for safety reasons. On our way Andrew showed me what he had also gotten from our mum. A silver ring with sapphire seashells decorated around it. Dad had given him, when I had left to go into the evil forest, he told me how dad wished he had given me the necklace.

I thought back to my first day back at home, when I had gotten a surprise visit from Etayo, Tafrikae and Kiola. Etayo had been forced by Tafrikae to bring them over, just to tell me their thanks for saving them, especially since I was well and in the privacy of my home. Kiola was now Tafrikae's guard for the people of Ulogboro, where she was awaiting her trial, to serve her time for the horror she had put them through, while she was Nameless.

After they had thanked me and checked me from head to toe that I was alright, they promised to visit me in future, and with that Etayo disappeared with them.

After they left, my friends also came over, so I had to go back down to meet them. Zina had dragged me away from the others, to give me a beautiful blue bracelet and to not forget I could always count on him to be there for me, if I needed him. He looked so sad, and I felt the same way because I couldn't possibly be his girlfriend or be with him now, even though he liked me and I would have liked to see how we would have been together.

'I hope Kion protects you in this new school of yours and I hope he is the right guy…for the job.' He added lamely after trailing off for a few seconds. He shook himself and smiled at me nervously, but decided it was time for us to return to the others.

He pulled me in for a hug and kissed me on the cheek, which was bittersweet. I wish he had kissed me on the lips again, but I knew it was pointless and better if we were just friends.

Mara engulfed me in a tight hug, which she didn't want to release me from, crying about how she was going to miss me so much, and how she wished she was a Geantoa so she could go with me. Her hug was so tight, she didn't want to let me go so I decided to be sly.

'Keep me updated, especially about you and him,' I said and glancing at Mike and back at her, she instantly let go off me in shock and she started blushing.

'You know?' she asked and gasped, a remorseful look on her face.

'Please! I know you Mara. I'm just disappointed you didn't talk to me bestie.' I said and she hugged me and apologized, promising to always send updates about her life.

Zoe came and took me away from Mara, she was fidgeting so I knew something was on her mind. 'I used to have a twin. She died and I lived.' She said meaningfully before hugging me and walking away. Her fear, it was her twin she was afraid of? I had to talk to her more about it later.

Everyone else had their time with me, hugging me and talking about different things before they all left, promising we would all stay in contact via social media. Thank God for the internet.

The school was at the outskirts of Lagos State, near Ogun State. There was only one in Nigeria and the population was very high, so I really hoped I would get to make new friends from different backgrounds, I was lucky I already had a friend in Kion and we were the same type of Geantoa.

I started to feel sleepy, when I looked out of the window and I saw the face of a woman who looked like my mum up in the cloud and she was smiling down at me. I drew Andrew's attention to the cloud but it had gone back to normal.

I looked at my necklace, the seashell resting on my chest and I smiled. My mum was always with me after all.

www.ingramcontent.com/pod-product-compliance
Lightning Source LLC
Chambersburg PA
CBHW030310160726
47992CB00005B/1951